MARK BATTERSON
AND JOEL N. CLARK

JACK STAPLES AND THE CITY OF SHADOWS

DAVID C COOK

transforming lives together

Madeleine True, Ethan Wylde, and Eva Blaze, thank
you for letting me tell you stories for so many years.
It made writing these books so much easier.

Elizabeth Esther and Amalie Megan, you will both go so far in
this life and I cannot wait to champion you along the way!

JACK STAPLES AND THE CITY OF SHADOWS
Published by David C Cook
4050 Lee Vance Drive
Colorado Springs, CO 80918 U.S.A.

Integrity Music Limited, a Division of David C Cook
Eastbourne, East Sussex BN23 6NT, England

The graphic circle C logo is a registered trademark of David C Cook.

This story is a work of fiction. All characters and events are the product of the author's
imagination. Any resemblance to any person, living or dead, is coincidental.

LCCN 2014948629
ISBN 978-0-8307-7596-5
eISBN 978-0-8307-7649-8

© 2015, 2018 Mark Batterson, Joel N. Clark
Published in association with the literary agency of The Fedd
Agency, Inc., Post Office Box 341973, Austin, Texas 78734.

The Team: Alex Field, Jamie Chavez, Nick Lee, Helen Macdonald, Karen Athen
Cover Design and Photos: Kirk DouPonce, DogEared Design; iStock

Printed in the United States of America
First Edition 2015

2 3 4 5 6 7 8 9 10

062918

Chapter 1

THE LIGHTNING DANCER

"It would be far easier to train an elephant to fly than to teach the heart," Mrs. Dumphry said, chuckling. "Can you imagine that?" She let out a great guffaw. "An elephant, flying! What a magnificent sight that would be. I wonder if any elephants have ever—" Mrs. Dumphry stopped. "What was I saying? Ah, that's right, you cannot instruct the heart. It must be awakened through experience. Just because you are one of the Awakened does not mean you are living fully awake …"

Jack Staples wasn't really listening to his ancient teacher; his eyes were glued to the sheer drop behind her. Mrs. Dumphry paced along the edge of a cliff without noticing when a toe or heel hovered over empty space.

Alexia Dreager was standing beside him, and he could tell she was furious. Jack hoped she wasn't going to start yelling at Mrs. Dumphry again; it never ended well when she did.

Arthur Greaves stood next to Alexia and was obviously afraid; he'd turned at least four shades of green in the last thirty seconds. Arthur was Jack's closest friend, and Jack knew Arthur wasn't afraid of heights. It was the water far below that captured his imagination. Arthur could barely swim a stroke.

Jack was getting a sinking feeling in the pit of his stomach. The past month had been filled with all sorts of crazy experiences. Mrs. Dumphry kept them busy doing some of the most ridiculous things Jack could have imagined.

They'd spent every day in "School for the Awakened," as Mrs. Dumphry called it. However, very little of what they did was like any school Jack had heard of. Mrs. Dumphry had them eating strange foods, reading poetry, singing songs, and learning language and dance. They'd spent a day climbing, another learning to juggle, and another cooking. They spent hours every day training with weapons and musical instruments.

Jack mostly trained with his black sword, Ashandar. Elion had told Jack it wasn't just a sword. It was also a teacher. The Sephari said it once belonged to the greatest Blades Master on earth, and if he could learn to surrender to it, Jack might also become great. Back in Ballylesson he'd felt Ashandar's power when he fought Oriax and killed a Shadule. The blade had been alive in his hands. Yet no matter how often he practiced with the thing, he'd never been able to repeat what happened.

Jack felt his chest tighten. That had been the day his mother died. He'd tried to save her and instead had gotten her killed. Jack shuddered. He could picture her lying in a sea of green grass. The Assassin had killed his mother, and Jack had been too weak to stop him.

Jack enjoyed learning the sword because he knew he would need it if he were going to kill the Assassin. But the rest of it was infuriating. Every time he asked why they were learning ridiculous things such as juggling or dance, Mrs. Dumphry would say something like, "Your imagination is a far more powerful weapon than a sword could ever be. If you learn the sword but have no imagination, your answer to every problem will be the sword."

Normally, Jack would have thought the whole thing a grand adventure. But his mother was dead and the city of Agartha had been destroyed. No matter what anyone said, he knew these things were at least partly his fault. To make matters worse, Jack's father and brother were missing, and he had no idea how to find them. Instead of searching for them or going back to bury his mother, or going anywhere at all for that matter, Jack and the others had been forced to wait in a small cottage somewhere outside of London. They'd arrived by boat a month earlier and had been waiting there ever since.

Mrs. Dumphry would tell them only that they were waiting word from Elion that it was safe to leave Great Britain. When they asked where they were going, she claimed not to know. Jack hated doing nothing. He was sure the Assassin wasn't sitting around playing childish games.

I could time travel … He immediately dismissed the thought. *No. I won't do it again. Not if I can help it.* Jack had walked through time, though he wasn't sure he'd be able to do it again, even if he wanted to. He'd gone back to save his mother's life. But not only had he been unable to save her, he'd hurt many others in the process.

Jack snapped back to attention. Mrs. Dumphry was standing with her back to the cliff, both heels hovering over empty space. A spattering of snow covered much of the ground, but Jack's shiver had nothing to do with the cold.

"What?" Arthur said with a moan.

"I said, I am going to count to three, then we will all jump together," Mrs. Dumphry repeated.

Jack struggled to catch his breath as his stomach churned, and looked over the edge. The cliff was impossibly high!

"I … I can't do it," Arthur stammered. "I'm not … I can't … the thing is, I'm not a good swimmer!" His eyes were wide. "I don't think I—"

"One!" Mrs. Dumphry's voice was a whip crack.

Arthur began talking faster. "It's just that I've never lived near water so I've only swum a couple of times, and I …"

"Mrs. Dumphry, I really don't think this is safe!" Jack added.

"Two!"

Arthur's hand shot to his mouth as he turned and promptly vomited his breakfast on a nearby rock.

"Isn't the water going to be freezing? I think Arthur is right. It's probably best that we come back another time," Jack said hastily.

"Three!"

Without another word, Mrs. Dumphry leaped from the edge and folded her body into a cannonball position. When she hit the water far below, the splash shot high into the air.

Alexia grimaced at Jack, then rolled her eyes at Arthur. "You really need to stop doing that. You're worse than a little girl." Without so much as glancing down, she dove from the edge, keeping her body perfectly straight with toes pointed. When she entered the water, there was almost no splash at all.

Far below, Mrs. Dumphry surfaced, cackling loudly. A moment later she looked up in confusion. "A rabbit with the heart of a lion is far more powerful than a wolf that believes itself a mouse." Beside her, Alexia bobbed up, looking pleased.

Jack thought he was going to hyperventilate. He knew they had to jump; Mrs. Dumphry would stay down there all day, if she had to. He glanced at Arthur and whispered, "It's going to be okay. She won't let you drown. Besides, if we wait, it will only make it worse, right?"

Jack closed his eyes and inhaled deeply. Screaming like a wild man, he ran off the top of the cliff. The fall lasted six and a half seconds, and as he surfaced, he gasped at the intensely cold water. Even still, he couldn't suppress a laugh. The fall had been exhilarating.

"Young Mr. Greaves," Mrs. Dumphry called, "my patience is wearing thin. You will jump now or I will throw you off."

"Come on, Arthur," Jack yelled. "It's really fun!"

Arthur took a step back, disappearing from view. "I can't do it!" he shouted.

Mrs. Dumphry *tsk*ed irritably, and a moment later, Jack heard a squeal from the top of the cliff. As he looked up, Arthur appeared. He was floating in midair and was screaming hysterically as he hovered over the edge. Mrs. Dumphry watched with a look of concentration.

Arthur kicked his legs frantically, flailing against something unseen as he dropped like a stone. A split second before he hit the water, twenty bolts of lightning streaked the sky.

Terror formed in the pit of Jack's stomach. Rock and earth rained down as he tried to look in every direction at the same time. Mrs. Dumphry offered Jack an amused smile, then turned back to Arthur.

Ten, twenty, thirty bolts lit up the sky, striking the lake or the nearby land. With each bolt that struck the lake, Jack felt as if he'd been kicked in the ribs. "We're under attack!" he yelled. "The Assassin is here!"

A short distance away, Arthur surfaced, thrashing wildly. "Help me!" he screamed.

"Arthur Reginald Greaves"—Mrs. Dumphry's voice was both commanding and reassuring—"you are safe! Face your fear, child. I will not let you drown."

Lightning struck just above Mrs. Dumphry's head, yet the bolt didn't hit her. Instead, it slammed against a shield of blue light.

"Help!" Arthur wailed.

"Fear is not real, boy." Mrs. Dumphry treaded water calmly. "It is a locked door. Face it and you will find the key."

Arthur barely kept his head above water as lightning rained down.

"We need to run!" Jack screamed. "The Assassin has come!"

"Arthur, you can do this!" Mrs. Dumphry's voice held a note of authority that cut through the chaos. "Look at me." Arthur locked eyes with her. "Child, you are courageous, you are strong, and you are able. And it is you who controls the lightning. Now, swim!"

A look of shock flashed across Arthur's face. He relaxed and began to dog-paddle as the lightning slowed and finally stopped.

Mrs. Dumphry grabbed his hand and raised him a little higher. "Arthur Greaves, I want you to strike that rock with lightning." She pointed to a large rock near the shoreline.

"What?" Arthur gasped. "It's not me! I can't …"

"Only a fool chooses blindness over sight," Mrs. Dumphry snapped. "Embrace what you know and become who you are meant to be. Besides, I would very much appreciate it if you would stop trying to hit me with your lightning and strike the rock instead."

Arthur stared at the rock as both fear and determination entered his eyes.

"You can do this. The lightning is part of you; it is as natural as breathing. You must—"

Crack! A bolt exploded into the rock. Arthur offered Mrs. Dumphry an incredulous look, then promptly fainted, slipping beneath the surface again. Mrs. Dumphry chuckled as she pulled him up and began swimming toward shore.

As she swam, she called back to Jack and Alexia. "Only when we face our fears will our greatest gifts be uncovered. We are not meant to control fear, but to defeat it."

Jack glanced at Alexia, who treaded water beside him. They shared an unbelieving look before swimming toward shore.

As he swam, Jack remembered the first time he'd seen lightning streak a cloudless night sky. A Shadule had been chasing him, when suddenly hundreds of bolts exploded throughout the forest, shattering trees and sending earth and stone flying.

Had the lightning come from Arthur?

When they reached shore, Jack was glad to see a fire already burning. Arthur sat nearby. He was shivering and staring wide-eyed at the shattered rock. Jack stayed silent and huddled close to the fire. Somehow Mrs. Dumphry's clothes and hair were completely dry. Her back was to the children, and she was staring into the forest. When Alexia arrived, Mrs. Dumphry turned.

"The Author has given each of you gifts that are specific to you. The reason we call the gift a Soulprint is because it is not something that can be learned; it is something that must be discovered. It was written on your soul the day of your birth." Mrs. Dumphry sat down next to the fire and warmed her hands. "Arthur's lightning is just one of his many gifts. Young Jack's ability to walk through time and Alexia's remarkable balance are merely the first Soulprints you have discovered."

"You keep talking about this Author," Alexia said irritably. "You and the rest of the Awakened claim to follow him, but why? Who is he? Have you even met him?"

"Yes, child. I have met him. More years ago than you could possibly imagine. But the Author is not from our world. He is from Siyyon, a world far from ours."

Jack searched his mind. Why did that name sound familiar? He was sure he'd heard it before.

"It was in Siyyon that the Assassin first attacked the Author," Mrs. Dumphry continued. "The war that followed was unlike any before. Millions died and much of Siyyon was destroyed."

Jack shivered.

"In the end, the Author and his followers defeated the Assassin and banished him. Many thousands of years later, the Assassin arrived here, in our world. Because Siyyon was forever lost to him, he decided to make earth his new home." Mrs. Dumphry smiled sadly. "Before long he took the form of a human and became the adviser to an evil queen. Together, the Assassin and the queen conquered much of the known world. And when the Author looked toward earth and saw what was happening, he was grieved. He …" Mrs. Dumphry stopped and turned to the forest. She tilted her head as if listening for something.

"Children, gather your things and do not dally." Her voice was tight. "Unless I miss my guess, the Assassin's servants have entered these woods, and …" She trailed off.

"What is it?" Jack asked.

"Be quiet, boy!"

For a long moment, no one moved. Jack strained his ears, listening for anything out of the ordinary, but there was nothing. Still, the longer they waited, the more the hairs on the back of his neck began to rise.

"It's a song," Arthur whispered.

The moment Arthur said it, Jack realized his friend was right. Jack did hear a song. It was faint but growing louder, as if a thousand songbirds were singing in harmony.

"It's so beautiful," Alexia whispered.

Mrs. Dumphry stood, a look of horror in her eyes. "Run, children! Run for your lives. No matter what happens, stay together and don't look back! Do you hear me? You must not look back! I will catch up as soon as I can."

Mrs. Dumphry grabbed Alexia and Arthur by the shoulders and shoved them forward. Jack watched both his friends disappear into the woods. *It's so beautiful!*

Jack blinked, realizing Mrs. Dumphry was standing in front of him. She was yelling, but he couldn't make out the words. He could barely make himself think of anything but the song.

Slap! Mrs. Dumphry smacked him hard across the face, then grabbed him by the shoulders. "Run, boy! Go now before you kill us all!"

As Jack turned to run, his wonder disintegrated into stark fear.

Chapter 2

THE MYZERAHL'S SONG

Alexia ran faster and harder than ever before. The dizzying song echoed throughout the forest. She tried to push it from her mind, but it was so bewitching she could barely think straight.

She glanced behind her, expecting to see Jack and Arthur, but no one was there. She stopped, suddenly afraid. Alexia knew she was a much faster runner than both boys, especially Arthur, but surely she should be able to see them! A branch snapped behind her.

Alexia gasped. Her mother was standing only a few paces away. She wore a beautiful yellow dress and was smiling. Tears welled in Alexia's eyes as she ran into her mother's arms.

"I have missed you terribly, my girl," her mother whispered. And though the song still boomed, Alexia barely heard it.

As she melted into her mother's embrace, something changed. It felt … wrong. A foreboding formed deep within her and Alexia opened her eyes. She screamed. It wasn't her mother she was hugging but a Shadule with a cruel scar crossing its face. The snakelike creature hissed as she leaped back.

"You thought you could kill me so easily?" the Shadule taunted. "I killed your father! I destroyed your home. You can never escape me!"

"No!" Hot tears slid down her cheeks. "No!" She knew she should run, but her feet were so heavy. The song reverberated around her, growing toward a crescendo.

"Where is my mother?" Alexia glanced around in confusion. *Wasn't she here just a moment ago?* It was a muddled thought. *No, that's not possible; she's been dead for years now.*

Alexia watched numbly as the Shadule's sinuous body bent bonelessly back, readying itself to strike.

Arthur Greaves was panicked. The hypnotic song thundered around him. Every note sent his heart leaping. But no matter how fast he ran, he couldn't keep up with Alexia. In a panic he glanced over his shoulder to be sure Jack was there.

Jack had stopped running. He was screaming at Arthur and waving his hands furiously. Whatever he was saying was lost in the roar of the song. Arthur motioned for Jack to hurry, but when he turned, he was surprised to see Mrs. Dumphry stalking toward him.

Why would Jack be afraid of Mrs. Dumphry?

"Arthur Greaves," Mrs. Dumphry said, "you have slowed us down for far too long. It is time for you to die." Without another word she released a spiderweb of fire. Arthur shrieked and dropped to the forest floor as the flames rocketed past.

Before Arthur could think what to do, Jack was standing over him with a look of pure murder. Jack knelt and punched Arthur hard in the face. *What's happening?*

"You're not like us!" Jack screamed. "You don't belong! And you're nothing but a coward!"

"Kill the boy," Mrs. Dumphry commanded. Jack nodded and grabbed a large rock.

Feeling desperate and hurt, Arthur leaped to his feet and ran.

Jack ran wildly, trying to catch up to Arthur. He knew he was faster, but no matter how fast he ran, Arthur managed to stay ahead. Jack glanced over his shoulder and was relieved to see no one was there. As he looked forward again, he skidded to a stop. Arthur had halted and was waving at Jack to hurry. Yet Arthur obviously hadn't seen the thick wall of slithering black fog rising from the ground just a few paces away.

Jack screamed and pointed at the fog, but he could barely hear his own voice over the thundering song. His head spun as the melody soared. Jack lurched forward to go help his friend, but he staggered to a stop as the Assassin strode out of the Shadowfog. The Assassin's cloak pulsed with dark light, and his skin sparkled like diamonds. His eyes were caverns of fire, and in his hand was a sword of white flame.

"I HAVE BEEN WAITING FOR YOU, BOY." The song changed as the Assassin spoke, the melody shifting to accompany the words. "I GAVE YOU THE CHANCE TO JOIN ME, BUT YOU TURNED YOUR BACK ON GREATNESS. NOW I WILL DESTROY YOU!"

Jack ran. His worst nightmare had come true. The Assassin had come for him.

Alexia closed her eyes, sure the Shadule would strike her at any second. Instead something crashed into her from behind, pinning her to the ground. She screamed. It was Arthur Greaves, lying on her and squealing like a girl.

"They're trying to kill me! Please, you have to help me!" He scrambled up. "They're coming!"

The world spun as Alexia stood. *What is he talking about?* Her head felt stuffed with wool. *Who's trying to kill him?* But Alexia knew she couldn't waste time thinking about Arthur. Something had been trying to kill her, hadn't it? *That's right—a Shadule!*

Alexia turned to see Jack screaming at a nearby tree. "Never!" he cried. "You killed my mother! I will never serve you!" Alexia began to laugh. *What is he doing? He looks like a madman!* Behind her Arthur wailed, "Please! No! I won't slow you down! I promise! I'll try to be brave. Just give me another chance!"

Alexia turned and almost fainted. Her father was standing in front of her. "I told you not to leave the house!" he shouted. She'd never seen her father angry before. "You could have saved us. It's your fault we died!"

Tears sprang to Alexia's eyes as she crumpled to the forest floor. At the periphery of her vision, she saw that Jack and Arthur had also dropped to their knees. All three children wept as the horrific song rose toward its final crescendo.

Alexia's father walked toward her and shifted, transforming into the scar-faced Shadule. Alexia knew she was about to die, but she was too heartbroken to care. Kneeling with their backs to her, both Jack and Arthur cowered low.

"Never!" Jack screamed.

"I'm sorry!" Arthur wailed.

The song cut without warning. And with the silence the Shadule evaporated. All three children gasped and fell breathless to the forest floor. For a long moment, the only thing Alexia could hear was the sound of all three of them choking back tears.

"What was that?" she said.

"Was it real?" Arthur whimpered. "Did it really happen?"

"What you saw was not real." Mrs. Dumphry strode through the trees. "But if the song had been allowed to finish, all of us would have died." She sat down and leaned heavily against a tree.

"A Myzerahl is not hard to kill if you can find it, but its song is death as sure as a sword in the belly." Mrs. Dumphry shook her head dizzily. "The Myzerahl takes your greatest fears, things you may not even know you feel, and uses them to destroy you."

Mrs. Dumphry closed her eyes and rubbed her temples. Alexia realized the old woman was as haunted as the rest of them. *She also must have seen something!* Alexia was happy at the thought, though she immediately felt guilty about it.

"How did you stop it?" Jack asked unsteadily.

"The only way to destroy a Myzerahl is to face your fears. And like all fear, once you have faced it, the battle is won."

"Are there any more of them out there?" Arthur didn't meet Mrs. Dumphry's eyes.

"No, child, there was only one. And we needn't fear another attack today. Dark servants never travel with the bird, for they, too, would be caught in its song. They send it ahead and follow far behind."

"What do you mean, bird?" Alexia asked.

"A Myzerahl is a bird … of sorts. Rather, it used to be a bird before it chose to serve the Assassin. The creature is not much larger than a blue jay and looks similar in shape and size." Mrs. Dumphry stood and brushed at her skirt. "Whether Elion is ready for us or not, we must leave England at once." She turned to face the children. "If all goes well, we will be safely on the other side of the world before the end of the day."

Chapter 3

WHEN EVERYTHING GOES WRONG

A few hours after the Myzerahl's attack, Mrs. Dumphry and the children arrived on horseback on the outskirts of London. Fresh snow began to fall as they neared the city. Just before they entered, Aias and Wild approached on horseback.

Aias reminded Jack of a wolf. The man moved with an impossible grace and always seemed ready to pounce. A wicked scar crossed his right eye and ended at his chin. And though he had lost half of his left arm in the battle of Agartha, it somehow managed to make him look more dangerous.

Wild rode next to Aias. The older boy had fierce, orange-tinged eyes and tight curls that sprouted in every direction. Wild was from the same town as Jack and Arthur. He was better with the bow and staff than anyone Jack had seen, but at best he looked like a wolf pup next to Aias.

Mrs. Dumphry had instructed the children to stay silent no matter what, so Jack merely nodded to the newcomers. He hadn't seen either of them since the battle of Agartha a month earlier and had no idea where they'd been since.

As they entered the city, Aias took the lead and Wild disappeared down a side street. The snowfall thickened as the sun sank low on the horizon. The golden light gave the city a truly magical look. Tall gas lanterns lined the streets, and almost every window shone with candle- or lamplight. Jack had never been to a big city and couldn't help but stare wide-eyed at absolutely everything. The long streets and grand buildings went on forever. For as long as he could remember, he had dreamed of visiting one of the great cities. His father had told many stories of Belfast, Dublin, and even London. And back then Jack had been desperate to have an adventure.

I don't want any more adventure, he thought bitterly. *I just want to go home. I want to stay in Ballylesson with Parker and Father and never leave again!*

Jack hadn't seen his brother or father for months now. They'd left Ballylesson the day after the circus fire to work in a nearby town. Jack's father was a stonemason, and both boys often worked alongside him. Mrs. Dumphry claimed that both his father and brother knew about the Awakened and Jack's role in the prophecy. But if that was true, why hadn't they said anything? It made Jack angry every time he thought about it. *If Father knew about the prophecy, why did he go? If he'd been there, he could have helped me save Mother!*

Just before the battle of Agartha began, Elion had promised Jack she would answer all of his questions. But he hadn't seen her since the battle.

Though Jack was consumed by his dark thoughts, another part of him could barely believe his eyes. London was enormous. He felt tiny as he craned his neck back to look up at a particularly tall building. Smoke rose from thousands of chimneys, and every street was wider than the widest street in Ballylesson. *How many people live here?* His mind spun at the thought. Thousands of people walked and rode everywhere. Everyone wore fancy clothes and spoke with funny accents. Yet as he made himself truly look, he began to feel a growing unease.

Something was wrong here. Two out of three people wore scarves covering their noses and mouths, and everyone seemed wary. And though people were everywhere, there was very little talking, and most spoke only in hushed whispers.

Equally unnerving were the words that had been scrawled on almost every street corner. "THE END OF THE WORLD IS NEAR. THE CHOICE MUST BE MADE. GET READY." Even Mrs. Dumphry appeared uneasy as she read the words.

How does one get ready for the end of the world? Jack wondered. *And what choice would you have to make?*

Aias zigzagged them through the city. It felt random. They often looped back to ride down the same street a second time. Every now and again Aias stopped for no reason Jack could see, and they would wait. A minute or so later, Wild would ride up from somewhere and whisper in his ear. Each time this happened, Aias shifted direction yet again.

After more than two hours of riding, Aias dismounted and strode inside a small shop connected to a horse stable. A wooden sign hanging above the door read, "Master Hampton's Coach Rental." As they dismounted, Jack realized Arthur was muttering beside him.

"What's wrong?" Jack whispered.

"I don't think I can do this," Arthur whispered back. "What about my parents? They must be worried sick. We keep going farther away! How will I ever see them again?"

Jack nodded. Arthur's words echoed his thoughts exactly. Mrs. Dumphry had promised both boys that, if it were possible, their families would be found and brought to them. But when they pressed for more information, she refused to say another word.

Each step took them farther from home. And though Jack didn't understand how it was possible, if Mrs. Dumphry was telling the truth, they would be on the other side of the world in just a few hours.

"I agree," Jack whispered, "but what can we do? The dark servants are chasing us. I don't think it's safe to go back to Ballylesson. Not after what happened there."

"I know they're chasing you and Alexia," Arthur said guiltily. "But I don't think they care about me. If I disappeared, Mrs. Dumphry wouldn't even notice!"

"Do you mean to leave us?" Jack asked anxiously. He didn't know what he would do if Arthur wasn't there.

"No," Arthur said. "Or, I don't know …" He whispered again. "I don't think Mrs. Dumphry has ever wanted me here. You and

Alexia are great at being heroes, but not me. I'm scared all the time. Everyone cares about what you do and where you go, but I'm just here because Wild found me and didn't think it safe to leave me behind. Mrs. Dumphry came to Ballylesson to get both of you. I just got caught up in it."

Before Jack could respond, Aias exited the coachman's shop. "Master Hampton has agreed to take us where we need to go," he said.

A tall man wearing a black coat and top hat offered a bow. "'Ello, young lords and ladies. Pleased to meet your acquaintance, I am!" Master Hampton bowed again.

"Reginald, Darby, and Hissey will ride in the coach with Lilly," Aias said. "We'll board the horses here while we're away."

Jack grimaced; Mrs. Dumphry had given each of them a new name to use in London. They were pretending to be the family of a high lord from somewhere up in the north of Ireland. Jack's name was Reginald, Arthur was Darby, and Alexia was Hissey. All three were meant to be Aias's children, though Aias was now Lord Blair, and Mrs. Dumphry was pretending to be their nanny. Jack had no idea who Wild was supposed to be.

"It is far too dangerous to use our real names," Mrs. Dumphry told them. "The Assassin's servants are everywhere these days. In the city they will be more numerous than rats."

Jack had lost count of how many rats he'd seen since entering London. The creatures scurried everywhere and seemed to have no fear of humans. *If the dark servants truly are more numerous …* He tried not to dwell on it.

"Reginald!"

Jack blinked. Mrs. Dumphry, Alexia, and Arthur were already inside the black lacquered coach, and all eyes were on Jack as he stood like a ninny in the falling snow. Aias mounted his stallion to ride alongside.

"Don't make your father tell you again! Get in!" Mrs. Dumphry's voice was sharp.

As he climbed into the coach, Jack saw a thick wall of white fog rolling toward them. Something about the fog didn't seem natural, but Mrs. Dumphry didn't look concerned so he decided not to mention it. As the coach lurched forward, Jack panicked. *We're truly leaving!* It had been impossibly hard to leave Ireland a month earlier, but leaving the United Kingdom altogether … Jack didn't want to think about it.

"In just a few minutes we will be inside Buckingham Palace," Mrs. Dumphry explained.

"What?" Jack and Arthur said on top of each other.

Mrs. Dumphry sighed as she offered the boys a withering look. "Until just a few hours ago, we didn't know how we would be leaving. The Council of Seven has been working tirelessly on four different escape plans. We can be sure the dark servants know about all of them, but it is our sincere hope they won't know which we have chosen until after we are gone."

"The dark servants know what we're doing?" Alexia said incredulously.

"This will go faster if I am not interrupted. Yes, I am sure the dark servants know all about our plans. And I am also sure they'll do everything in their power to stop us. But since they don't know which way we will run, they will have to divide their forces. We will travel by way of a World Portal." Mrs. Dumphry held up her hands to halt any interruptions. "It's a way of traveling a great distance in a few steps. We had one in Agartha, but it was destroyed when the city fell. There are four more scattered throughout Great Britain. The portal we have chosen is inside the palace, located just below the dungeons. Andreal and Miel are already inside and have a plan to take us to the portal without being seen."

Jack felt a pang of fear. "Andreal wants to kill me. He thinks I will serve the Assassin. How could you trust him?"

Mrs. Dumphry fixed Jack with a cold stare. "Andreal was misguided in his desire to kill you, I admit," she said. "But he is a giant, and giants are often hasty and quick-tempered. They are also fiercely loyal, and I promise you, he can be trusted."

Jack didn't care what Mrs. Dumphry said. The giant hated him. The prophecy that spoke of Jack and Alexia said a lot of strange things. But part of it said that at least one of them would bow before the Assassin and destroy the world. Andreal had been sure Jack was that child, and his answer had been to kill Jack so he'd never have the chance.

The prophecy said, "The child will both destroy the world and save it." It also said, "The child will bow before the Assassin and defeat him once and for all." It didn't make a lick of sense. Until recently everyone had thought there was only one child, but now there were two. While every human in the history of the world had been born with invisible scales covering their eyes, Jack and Alexia had been born without them. This apparently meant they both were "the Child of Prophecy."

"If all goes well, we will be through the portal within the hour," Mrs. Dumphry continued. "If all does not go well"—she hesitated—"no matter what happens, I need you to stay with me and do exactly as I say. We must not be separated!"

Mrs. Dumphry reached into a bag and pulled out two brown cloaks. "These are Atherial Cloaks. They are a gift from Elion. When you wear them, you are almost invisible."

Jack squinted at the cloaks. They didn't look like anything special.

"The cloak will also act as a shield and will block a sword or spear thrust, so long as it is not a direct hit," Mrs. Dumphry said. "Each is worth more than all the gold in London." She handed one cloak to Jack and the other to Alexia and didn't seem to notice Arthur's disappointed look.

"If you have any questions, now would be the time to ask," Mrs. Dumphry said briskly.

"Where will the World Portal take us?" Jack asked. It seemed the only question that mattered.

"I do not know."

"What's that supposed to mean?" Alexia said.

"It means what it means, child. We are searching for the Forbidden Garden, but the garden is never in the same place and is always moving."

Aias leaned into the coach window. "We're nearly there," he said in a hushed voice. Arthur jumped at Aias's unexpected appearance, then blushed. Aias rolled his eyes. "Once we're in the gates, stay together. Anyone could be a dark servant, and those who aren't are almost as dangerous."

When Aias closed the curtain, Arthur whispered, "Is Elion going to help us?"

Mrs. Dumphry smiled. "She already is, child. You didn't think all this fog was natural, did you?"

A minute later someone shouted outside. "Halt in the name of King Edward! Who are you and what are you doing here this time of night?" The carriage stopped abruptly as Mrs. Dumphry placed a finger to her lips.

Jack pulled the curtain aside to peek out.

"I said stop, stranger!" The shouting man had a thick beard and wore the red and black uniform of the King's Guard. Jack and Arthur shared a fearful look as he unsheathed his sword. Aias nudged his stallion steadily forward.

"Take one more step and I'll be forced to arrest you!"

"In a dream, everything seems possible," Aias said. "But it is only after we awaken that we can truly live the impossible."

The guard gaped for a moment, then turned and shouted. "Open the gates! Open them now or I'll dock a month's pay from each of you!"

The guard stepped forward hesitantly. "M'lord, I know it's not my place to ask," he said in a low voice, "but is it true? Has the Child of Prophecy been born? Is the Last Battle nearly here?"

Aias stared at the man but didn't answer.

"It's just that … with everything that's been happening, I … I thought …" The man trailed off.

"The Last Battle is not far off," Aias said. "And it is not one child who was born, but two."

The guard gasped, but before he could say anything, Aias continued. "Stand strong. We will need every last sword in the coming days. Continue to gather the Lambs." Aias glanced at the unearthly fog. "We must go now. We've lingered too long already." He raised his voice slightly. "Master Hampton, if you are done with your eavesdropping, would you kindly continue through the gate?"

Jack heard the coachman yelp as the carriage lurched forward. "What does he mean, 'the Last Battle'?" Jack whispered. Mrs. Dumphry merely placed a finger to her lips to silence him.

Another minute passed and the group exited the carriage to a thick wall of white fog and heavy snow. Jack shivered as the fog touched his skin. Did it feel different or was he just imagining it?

"Halt. Who goes there?" Two sword-bearing guards appeared out of the fog, stalking toward Aias. "How did you get inside the palace grounds?"

Aias smiled. "My good sirs, I assure you everything is in order. We were given permission to enter by—"

Without warning, both men charged with swords bare. Aias moved like a snake, and before Jack knew what was happening, the men were on the ground. Aias hadn't even bothered to unsheathe his sword. "It's a trap!" he grunted. "It has to be. Miel should have been waiting for us, not these louts. All our planning has been for nothing!"

"We need to—" Mrs. Dumphry stopped as something rumbled from high above. "No!" She gasped.

"It can't be," Aias groaned.

Boom! A thunderclap exploded as a torrent of wind forced back the unnatural fog. Instantly, a perfect circle of clear air formed in the center of the courtyard. When his eyes landed on the monster, Jack began to scream.

Mrs. Dumphry raised her arms as she stepped forward. "We've been betrayed!" she screamed as a ball of fire exploded from her hands. "It's a Drogule!"

Chapter 4

THE MONSTER IN
THE COURTYARD

A particularly large flake of snow landed on Alexia's nose and immediately melted. Yet Alexia didn't notice the snow; all her attention was on the monster hulking on the other side of the square. Mrs. Dumphry had called it a Drogule, but it was a monster pure and simple. It was gigantic, standing almost as tall as the palace.

A vast horde of dark servants had gathered just behind the monster. There were two Shadule and at least three hundred Oriax. The Shadule were sleek, almost graceful creatures; the Oriax were a mixture of mammal and reptile, the size of a small pony. Yet it was the monster that most captured Alexia's attention. The Drogule's body was stone, and its mouth was ringed in metallic fangs.

Alexia groaned as the monster spoke in a voice like an avalanche. "Kill all but the child we seek."

Without hesitation the mass of dark servants surged forward. The two Shadule dropped to the paving stones and slithered ahead as the Oriax leaped toward the small band of Awakened.

"Stay close!" Mrs. Dumphry screamed, sending fifty threads of fire exploding from her fingers. For a brief moment, Alexia shared a fearful look with Jack and Arthur. Hundreds of dark servants and a monster were charging at six Awakened, and yet Mrs. Dumphry wanted them to stand and fight. Had the old woman lost her mind?

"Follow me!" Jack screamed, and at the same time, Arthur shouted, "This way!" And just like that, both boys fled from the coming charge. Alexia watched them go, hesitating only a moment before deciding they had the right of it. She was always up for a fight, but these were impossible odds and only a fool would choose to stay.

Alexia made it only a few steps before skidding to a stop. One of the Shadule had slithered around the back of the courtyard and was now directly in front of her. It rose fluidly, and its milky white eyes fixed on Alexia. "Come with me, girl," it said. "The master has great plans for you." The Shadule extended a clawed hand and offered a sickly smile as wings unfurled from its body.

Alexia wanted to scream. She had killed one of these creatures a month earlier, but it had almost killed her in the process. *I need to buy some time!* she thought, then schooled her face and smiled, offering a quick curtsy. "Why, thank you, Mr. Shadule," she said.

"I would be ever so happy to accept your invitation to meet your master. Please, would you take me to him?"

The Shadule hissed, momentarily confused by Alexia's pleasant agreement. It looked around as if expecting a trap, and in that moment, Alexia swung her sling with all her might. The Shadule howled as the stone struck it square on the forehead.

Alexia darted away, sprinting toward a small wooden door at the side of the courtyard. She knew a stone could never kill a Shadule, but if she was lucky, she'd gained a few precious seconds. *I can't believe that worked!* As she ran, she loosed another stone at an Oriax that appeared in front of her.

The beast dropped, dead before it hit the ground. *The only way to kill an Oriax is to strike it directly between the eyes.* Mrs. Dumphry's words from weeks earlier echoed in her mind. As she leaped over the beast, she spotted ten more galloping to intercept her. Her heart sank as she glanced back to see the Shadule slithering behind.

A thought struck Alexia like a fist to the face. *The Atherial Cloak! How could I have forgotten?* She'd stuffed the thin material into the inside pocket of her own cloak.

The beasts stampeded toward her, and Alexia shifted her direction so she was running straight at them. She screamed as she grabbed the Atherial Cloak and vaulted high into the air. *Just pretend you're in the circus*, she thought as she twisted her body, wrapping the thin material around herself in midair.

The four closest beasts jumped at Alexia with teeth bared. As she disappeared, the Oriax screeched. Alexia navigated between them, missing them by a hair. When the beasts landed, they slammed into the Shadule that had been close on her heels.

Alexia rolled to her feet and continued her mad dash toward safety. "That was too close!" she said breathlessly as she darted past more Oriax. The Atherial Cloak seemed to be working. None of the beasts had noticed her passing. As she approached the door, she looked back in hopes of finding Jack or Arthur, yet all she saw was Mrs. Dumphry and Aias.

The old woman moved like a hurricane, leaping, spinning, and somersaulting continuously, each movement sending spiderwebs of fire into the attacking horde. Aias fought beside her, his sword wreathed in flames. When it connected with flesh, the dark servants crumbled to dust. The two Awakened stood their ground against the onslaught of hundreds of Shadow Souled.

The Drogule was on the opposite end of the courtyard, smashing fists through pillars and roaring angrily.

"Jack!" Alexia's breath caught at the sight of her friend diving away from the Drogule's huge fist. Another pillar crumbled and Jack dove behind some rubble in an attempt to hide.

Alexia scanned the square. It was filled to bursting with dark servants, and even with the Atherial Cloak, it would be impossible to cross. But Jack was backed into a corner with nowhere to hide. Alexia wanted to scream as the Drogule raised both fists high.

Suddenly, a piercing voice sounded from somewhere above. It was so pure and strong that it penetrated the chaos below. For a brief moment the fighting stopped and the courtyard became still. Man, creature, monster, and beast gazed toward the heavens.

A small figure hovered above the square. Her hair spread above her like a fan and glowed with a golden light. Her eyes were a thunderstorm, and as she sang, each word shattered the night. Alexia couldn't understand the language, but it didn't matter. The song was filled with such sorrow and loss that she wanted to weep.

"Elion!" Alexia whispered. The Sephari's voice was beautiful and terrifying beyond words. Every eye stayed pasted to the sky. As Elion stretched out her arms, wisps of colored mist began rising from paving stones and walls.

The dark servants shied away from the mist as stones burst free and shot upward to spin slowly around Elion. Alexia didn't move. It was mesmerizing. Stone and earth splintered from the ground, adding to the otherworldly tornado. Even the black lacquered coach bolted upward. Alexia saw the coachman, Master Hampton, lying flat on his back, clutching his eyes as if the light were too bright. *The poor man must have been hiding under the coach!*

Gradually the battle began again, and Alexia was about to flee when something grabbed her from behind and began hauling her backward.

She shrieked as she was dragged through an open doorway and dropped to the ground. Alexia scrambled to her feet and saw Wild closing the door. "What are you doing just standing there?" he shouted. "That cloak doesn't make you totally invisible, you know!"

Slam! Alexia's fist connected solidly with Wild's jaw. "Don't ever do that again!" she growled. "I was coming if you had just waited a second, you sheep-head!"

Wild rose to his feet, probing his jaw tenderly. "You punched me! What's wrong with you?"

"Maybe I don't like being dragged about and thrown to the ground!"

"Whatever Elion is doing," Wild said, "it's not some fireworks show on Guy Fawkes Day. You can't just sit and watch like a country bumpkin!"

Alexia balled her fists. Of anyone she'd met, Wild knew the quickest way to get under her skin. The boy was infuriating. She was about to hit him again when the wooden door burst open. Both children leaped back as four Oriax tried to enter the passageway at the same time, momentarily becoming stuck in the doorway. The beasts squealed and brayed as they tried to flee whatever was happening outside.

"I know you want to punch me again"—Wild offered a half grin—"but it might be best if we run now." He darted down the darkened passageway without another word.

Alexia was furious. Had he really just grinned at her? As the two children rounded a corner, they skidded to a stop. "Get down!" Wild screamed. Alexia shrieked when she saw the cannon aimed directly at them.

Boom!

Alexia dropped and threw her body back as the cannonball whizzed overhead. The noise was deafening and the air instantly filled with dust and debris. For a long moment, she didn't move but stared upward, catching her breath. Her ears rang and she was dizzy. When she finally struggled to her feet, Alexia was exceedingly woozy.

The cannonball had burst through the back wall, shot across the courtyard, and exploded through a wall on the opposite side. Alexia leaned heavily against the ruined wall and rubbed at her temples. Inside the square the battle still raged. Mrs. Dumphry and Aias stood back-to-back, fighting impossible odds. Alexia could no longer see the Drogule or hear Elion's electrifying song. She closed her eyes and tried to regain her senses. As her hearing slowly returned, she realized someone was screaming.

"You nearly killed us all, you blooming fool!" Whoever was talking was obviously angry. "Lieutenant Greyfield gave strict instructions: you were not to fire unless we knew the child would not be harmed!" Alexia turned to see a leather-faced man yelling at a much younger man. Both wore the uniform of the King's Guard.

"I'm sorry, Captain," the man said. He raised his arms defensively. "I thought they were—"

The captain slugged the man hard in the stomach. "I didn't give you permission to speak."

Alexia suddenly remembered she hadn't been alone when the cannon went off. She scanned the rubble and barely suppressed a scream. Wild was lying on his back, covered in debris. His forehead was smeared with blood, and she couldn't tell if he was breathing.

"There!" The captain pointed at Wild. "Bring the boy to me, and find his companion!"

Alexia froze, confused. Two of the guards walked directly past. *What's happening?* She held her breath as she waited for the men to attack, but they merely carried Wild back to the captain.

You're wearing the Atherial Cloak, you goat-headed ninny! Alexia flushed. This was the second time she'd forgotten about the cloak. More of the guards passed within inches as they searched the rubble. Alexia was careful not to move.

"There's no one here, sir," one of the guards called.

"Impossible!" the captain snarled. "The boy was speaking to someone. Keep looking!" As the leather-faced captain walked toward the rubble, Alexia almost screamed. The man walked with a heavy limp. *What on earth is he doing here?* Alexia could barely believe it. She knew the man—he'd tried to kidnap her when she was just seven years old!

Six years and three months earlier

The endless, hypnotic sound of hooves plodding on dirt changed suddenly. And with the change, new smells filled the air and a steady clamor began to rise. With every passing second, the world grew louder and more vibrant.

From beneath the pile of straw, Alexia Dreager opened her eyes. She'd awoken from the same dream she had every night. But for once, she didn't care about the dream. "I made it!" she whispered, hardly able to believe it. Alexia grinned. Although she couldn't see a thing, the sounds and smells were mesmerizing. Cautiously, she began wriggling out from beneath the straw.

"Are you going to leave without saying good-bye, then?"

Alexia froze. *Is he talking to me?*

"I don't mind you napping in my wagon, but it would be rude to leave without at least giving me your name."

Alexia had been sure the leathery old farmer hadn't seen her sneak into his wagon. With a sigh, she climbed upward and readied herself to flee in case he tried to capture her. But she promptly forgot all about the farmer. With hay sticking to hair and clothes, her jaw dropped as she tried to look in every direction at once. It was magnificent!

The farmer chuckled. "I take it this is your first time to Belfast?"

Alexia ignored him. She had never imagined anything so grand. *So many people!* The sight took her breath away. The sun had only begun to rise, but even so, there were at least one hundred people walking or riding along the cobblestone street.

The surrounding buildings were monstrous, rising seven stories and making Alexia feel as small as an ant. It was grander than anything she'd imagined. She had dreamed of going to Belfast for years now. She was only seven, but her father told her all about the majestic city when she was just four years old.

"Belfast is the grandest city in all Ireland," he'd said. "Ah, my Alley Goat, you will love it!"

Alexia frowned at the memory, pushing back tears. She'd been sitting in her father's lap. She remembered it perfectly. His beard brushed against the top of her head and his arms were wrapped tightly around her.

"I want to go now!" she'd demanded.

"Patience, my little goat. I will take you there someday, I promise."

Alexia grimaced at the memory. He would never be able to keep that promise. Less than a year later, he and Alexia's mother had died in a fire. *You shouldn't make promises you can't keep*, she thought bitterly.

"Are you all right, child? You don't look well."

Alexia abruptly realized the old farmer had been talking to her. Flustered, she yelped and ducked beneath the hay. The man let out a great guffaw. "It's okay. I am glad you're here. Even if we didn't talk last night, it's always nice to know someone is nearby. It makes the darkness far less lonely."

Alexia surfaced again. "How did you know I was here?" she asked as she scanned the city.

"That red dress makes you easy to spot," the farmer said, smiling. "And even if I hadn't seen the dress, I'd have heard the snoring. You were as loud as a pig digging for truffles."

"I don't snore!" Alexia glared at the man as she fingered the hem of her dress. Her mother had made it for her and she hadn't taken it off since the first day she'd tried it on. She even bathed in the thing. It had been given to her on her fifth birthday, which was the same day her parents had died. Somehow, the dress still fit perfectly. Alexia assumed it must have stretched out. Though it should have been worn through and filled with holes, it still looked as good as new.

The wrinkled old farmer chuckled as he reached into his satchel. "I suppose I must have been mistaken about the snoring. A wee girl like you could never have made such a thunderous noise!" The man offered a large loaf of bread. "My wife baked it yesterday; would you like it?"

Alexia's stomach rumbled as she eyed the loaf. She'd had very little to eat in the past few days, and never in her life had she been offered an entire loaf all to herself. "It's all right. You can have it, if you like. I'm not feeling all that hungry, and you look like you could do with a little fattening up." As Alexia reached for the loaf, she looked up at the farmer and smiled.

The farmer jerked back. "No!" he gasped and looked around feverishly. "It's not possible!" He lurched forward and seized her by the wrist, twisting it at an awkward angle. Alexia cried out as his leathery fingers lifted her chin so he could clearly see her eyes. "It's you!"

Alexia tried to scream, but her voice caught as the farmer twisted her arm back even farther. He licked his lips hungrily. "My reward will be beyond measure," he muttered and then looked around as if expecting a trap. "Where are your protectors, girl? Where are the Awakened?"

Alexia was sure her arm was about to snap. "Please let go." She sobbed. "I didn't do anything!"

The man abruptly seemed to remember they were in the middle of a crowded street. "Be quiet! Answer me truthfully or I'll do far worse than break your arm. Where are your protectors?"

Alexia shook her head. She had no idea what the man was talking about. She shifted painfully.

"Scream, and it will be the last thing you do," the farmer whispered as he released her arm and grabbed her roughly by the shoulders. "The Shadow Souled have searched through the ages." He trembled as spittle dripped from his chin. "And here you are! You came to me, to my wagon!"

He's a madman! Alexia's mind spun as she tried to make sense of it.

"Perhaps I will serve in Thaltorose itself!" the man said. "Tell me the truth, girl; are you the prophesied one? Are you the child we've been waiting for?"

"Please let me go. Please!" She trembled. "I didn't do anything!" Alexia closed her eyes and squeezed her fists tight. "Please!" Suddenly a strong wind ripped at her clothes as the wagon jerked forward, and the man wailed and loosened his grip. Alexia opened her eyes to see the farmer fall off the side. She was barely able to keep her footing as the wagon lurched to a stop.

For a moment, she didn't move. *What just happened?* The farmer lay on the ground with one leg bent at an impossible angle. His horse had collapsed to the ground as if dead.

Alexia looked around. Everyone on the street had stopped to watch. She turned and jumped from the side and darted away. As she ran, she noticed two more horses and a goat that also lay, unmoving, on the ground.

Chapter 5

A SHABBY PEN

Present day

The Drogule roared and leaped upward in an attempt to reach Elion. Yet the Sephari hovered just out of reach, taunting the monster with her otherworldly song. Jack let out a relieved breath. Had Elion not arrived, the Drogule would have smashed him to a pulp. There had been no more pillars to hide behind.

Jack darted beneath the Drogule and raced to a wooden door in the side of the palace. *Locked! What now?* Then he froze. An Oriax with the body of a tiger and the head and shoulders of a bear was directly in front of him. Jack jumped away as the beast bounced off the locked door and turned, growling. Jack scrambled back and threw a rock at its head, but the Oriax didn't even blink as the stone bounced away. As it stalked closer, Jack had nowhere left to run. He threw another rock, then swung his satchel. The Oriax snatched the leather bag out of the air with its teeth.

Jack glanced up at Elion in desperation. The Sephari still hovered above the square. Her hair glowed like the sun as stone, earth, and carriage spun round her in a tempest. She met Jack's eyes and offered a tight smile. As the Oriax leaped, Elion dropped her arms, and the spinning bricks and stones crashed into the dark army below.

Every Oriax near Jack was slammed aside by paving stone and brick, and throughout the square the beasts howled. The Drogule raged as the carriage collided with it, knocking the monster to its knees. Before it could rise, something exploded across the courtyard.

Boom!

The wall opposite Jack burst apart; a cannonball shot through the square and crashed into the Drogule. The monster let out a colossal roar as it shattered into a thousand stony pieces. Even as the Drogule died, the cannonball continued its flight and shattered the door Jack had just tried to open.

Jack shivered. Had he been standing one pace to the left, the cannonball would have removed his head from his shoulders. His legs felt like water as he stepped into the palace and ran down a dark corridor.

Five minutes later, Jack had not stopped running. He stormed through a passageway filled with elaborate tapestries and life-size statues. He'd passed three palace servants and one old woman who wore pajamas and shrieked, "Good heavens, child, slow down!"

When he finally stopped, Jack gasped for breath. He had no idea where he was or what he would do next. *Stop running like a madman!* he thought as he slowed his breathing. *Try to blend in!*

He pulled his cloak over the pommel of his sword to hide it, and stopped. *The Atherial Cloak!* It was in the satchel he'd hurled at the Oriax. He wanted to kick himself for being so stupid. *If I had it now, I could use it to …* Jack stood perfectly still, holding his breath. He was standing directly in front of two guards. Both men were seated, with their heads leaning heavily against the wall.

Jack stepped closer and saw that both guards were sleeping. Unable to believe his luck, he tiptoed down the corridor until he heard voices coming from somewhere up ahead. He circled back the way he had come and saw the silhouettes of three sword-bearing men walking toward him. Jack was trapped as sure as a rabbit in a snare.

Holding his breath again, he tiptoed between the two guards and pushed on the door. When it swung soundlessly inward, Jack crept inside and closed it. *From the snare straight into the pot!* he thought. The chamber was enormous and lit by dozens of torches and three fire pits. At its center, a number of men in full military uniform were leaning over a table, studying a map.

A younger man, with black hair and three stripes on the arm of his uniform, spotted Jack. "Who are you, boy, and how did you get past the guards?"

Jack jumped. He opened his mouth but couldn't think of anything to say.

"Speak, or I'll have your hide," the man threatened.

"T-the palace is u-under attack," Jack stammered. He was far too flustered to think of a good enough lie, so he decided it might be best to tell the truth. "I was trying to hide. But I didn't mean to interrupt. I'll just leave now. So sorry!"

"My boy," an older, gray-haired gentleman said. "There's no need to be afraid. We are not under attack. My lieutenant has been planning a surprise training exercise for the King's Guard. I am sure this is what you saw. But I do need you to answer truthfully—how did you get past the guards and into my war chamber?"

Jack looked at the older man and made a decision. "Sir, there is something evil in the courtyard …' It's chasing me and my friends, and it's not a training exercise. Even now, some of the palace is being destroyed." The older man's eyes widened.

"Preposterous!" A sandy-haired man stepped forward and offered Jack a scornful look. "Will someone get this boy out of our sight? He has wasted enough of our time." The man turned to the older gentleman. "I am sorry, Your Majesty. But this boy is clearly delusional. I will question him myself when we are through here."

It's the king! Jack was suddenly breathless. *It's King Edward!*

"Lieutenant Greyfield," the older man said, "unless I am mistaken, I am the one who gives commands here. And sometimes it is the delusional who see most clearly." He gave Jack a grandfatherly smile. "My dear boy, have no fear. So long as you speak the truth, no harm will come to you. Now, come here so I can get a better look at you."

The raven-haired man who'd first spotted Jack stepped forward. "My king, may I suggest you don't allow the child to come too close? He may be a boy, but he is hiding a sword beneath that cloak."

"General Blair." The king offered a tired sigh. "I am surrounded by the best soldiers in all of Britain. And you may remember I also am none too shabby with a blade." He looked at Jack and narrowed his eyes. "Child, I am not used to asking the same question more than once."

Jack let out a long breath. Every eye was on him as he approached the king, and Jack abruptly realized he should probably bow or something. He dropped to his knees awkwardly as he realized he had no idea how to bow.

"Your Majesty, please, I'm not lying! There are monsters in the courtyard and even now they may be stalking the halls of your palace."

The king stepped closer and knelt before Jack, lifting his face to the light. As he did, Jack saw the tiniest smile creep onto the king's lips. The king turned to his men. "The palace is under attack. Go now and rally the men."

"Your Majesty, you can't be serious!" Lieutenant Greyfield erupted. "You would take the word of a child?"

"And take Lieutenant Greyfield to the dungeons," the king said. "He has betrayed the crown."

Without warning, Lieutenant Greyfield drew his sword and lunged at Jack. Yet King Edward moved like a viper, drawing his own sword and deflecting Greyfield's away. Greyfield fell at Jack's feet.

The king placed the tip of his sword against the lieutenant's back so he couldn't move. It all happened so quickly that none of the other men had so much as reached for their swords. All were shocked as they looked from the king to Greyfield.

"We have been betrayed, gentlemen." The king spoke in a commanding voice. "Hear me! This attack does not come from normal men. All of you know of the dark happenings this past month, man

and animal going insane and people disappearing by the thousands."
King Edward glared at Lieutenant Greyfield, who didn't dare move
for fear of being run through.

"Tonight's attack comes from the same darkness that's been
spreading throughout our land. Do not trust your eyes; trust your
instincts. Even a mangy dog may be deadly. Now go; rally the King's
Guard and defend the palace!"

Two men began dragging Greyfield out of the war chamber.
"You won't escape, boy! The Shadow Lord demands your death for
what you did! No matter where you run, we will find you! We are
in every city and every kingdom. The end is near and the darkness
is coming, night without end, Quagmire's—" The doors to the war
chamber closed, and Greyfield was silenced at last.

The king turned to Jack. "Well now, that was rather unpleasant!"
He smiled warmly. "The Author be praised! I am most honored to
meet you, my dear boy."

The king reached into his jacket pocket and carefully fished out a
small leather pouch. He opened it to reveal an ancient-looking feathered pen. "This has been in my family for thousands of years," the
king said solemnly. "We have kept it safe, as we were commanded."
He bowed his head.

Jack looked from the pen to King Edward, unsure what was
happening.

"Well," the king said, "aren't you going to take it?"

"What is it?" Jack asked, utterly perplexed.

"It's a pen, of course! Beyond that, I honestly have no idea. I'd
hoped you might be able to tell me."

Jack took the pen, shaking his head.

"I assume it must be important in our war against the Assassin," the king said. "If it doesn't mean anything now, I have no doubt it will be of the utmost importance in the future."

The feather was worn and shabby, and the quill so dry and cracked that it would make a terrible pen. Besides seeming ancient, it didn't look any different from other feathered pens Jack had seen. He placed the pen back in the leather pouch, then inside his jacket pocket, wondering if King Edward might not be fully sane.

The king let out a long breath as he watched it disappear. "All I can tell you is that my family was commanded to keep the pen safe until you came to us. And we have faithfully waited these thousands of years."

Jack just stood there, unsure if he should say thanks or something of the sort.

"Now, we haven't much time." The king turned and walked toward a corner of the war chamber. "If the attack has made it into the palace, then I assume someone has betrayed you. Let's get you to the World Portal before it's too late, shall we?"

Chapter 6

THE GANG OF TERROR

Alexia had followed the leather-faced captain for almost an hour. After more twists and turns than she could count, she was no closer to rescuing Wild. *Wake up, you wool-head!* She willed Wild to regain consciousness. *You can't expect me to save you and carry you!*

Every time Alexia looked at the captain, a shiver ran down her spine. She'd tried to forget that morning in Belfast when the farmer had almost kidnapped her. Yet now that she thought about it, it had only been when he'd seen her eyes that he'd changed. He must have known then that Alexia was one of the Children of Prophecy. Somehow that same farmer had become a captain of the King's Guard.

With the Atherial Cloak to hide her, Alexia thought she might be able to use her sling to knock out six or seven of the men before they knew what hit them. But she definitely couldn't take all fifteen. In the meantime, she kept a close eye on Wild. She would need his help if she were going to properly rescue him.

At any other time, Alexia would have gawked. Buckingham Palace was beyond anything she'd imagined. The corridors went on forever and were filled with elaborate tapestries and impressive statues. But she didn't care about any of it. All she wanted was to rescue Wild and get safely away. *If the boy doesn't wake up soon*, she thought irritably, *I'll punch him in the nose!*

The captain abruptly stopped and turned to his men. "You lot stay here and stop anyone who tries to follow. The two of you"—he motioned to the men dragging Wild—"follow me." He turned and stalked down a dark stairwell. Even with a limp, he was surprisingly quick.

This may be my chance! Alexia darted past the guards. She should be able to knock out all three men. She placed a stone in the fold of her sling and readied herself as she followed the captain down a seemingly endless staircase.

I bet they're taking Wild to the dungeons! Mrs. Dumphry had brought them here to use something called a World Portal—she'd said it was located just below the dungeons. Alexia decided to hold off. She would allow the men to carry Wild down. If they stopped at the dungeons, she would knock them out and carry him the rest of the way; if they led her to this World Portal, even better.

The deeper they descended, the rougher the walls became, shifting from brick and mortar to hewn stone. When they finally reached the bottom, the captain knocked loudly on a small metal door. As the door opened, Alexia almost hissed. She knew the young man standing on the other side. His name was Petrus, and he was the cruelest boy she'd ever met.

"Who's this, then?" Petrus growled, looking as if he'd sucked on a lemon.

"He's one of them," the captain said. "Now move aside before I skin your hide for slowing us."

Petrus's grimace deepened, but he stepped back and allowed the men through. Just as he was about to close the door, Alexia loosed her stone so it ricocheted off a nearby wall. As Petrus turned to look, she slipped past him.

When she saw the group of young men and women waiting on the other side, she almost fainted. Alexia knew all of them. By the looks of it, every last member of the Gang of Terror was here. Alexia was as tense as a bowstring.

Six years and two months earlier

Alexia had entered the grand city with excitement welling in her heart, but it hadn't taken long to realize that Belfast was a dangerous place. It was nothing like her father had explained. Or maybe it was better to say that there were two, very different worlds within the city.

In one world, everything was bright and clean. The people were well dressed and spoke in a proper-sounding accent. They went about their daily business without seeming to notice the world boiling just beneath.

Those who lived in the second world were a far more cunning and dangerous lot. They made their homes in the back alleys and sewers of the city. They were purse-snatchers, cutthroats, thieves, and urchins; they were vagrants and vagabonds, and they ruled the night. People from the first world who found themselves on the streets past dark were usually lucky if they still had their smallclothes by morning.

Stealing and fighting were the only rules that mattered in the second world. The wealthy pretended not to notice the urchins unless they were standing face-to-face. If this happened, they would either toss a few pence or call the police. Yet the police were the cruelest of them all. Those they arrested were usually never seen again.

In the past weeks Alexia had narrowly escaped being robbed, beaten, and arrested. She spent her nights sleeping on the rooftops, wrapped tightly in a blanket she'd stolen from a washing line. She'd learned quick enough that the higher she went, the safer she was. No one else seemed to want to sleep on the rooftops.

Alexia knew she couldn't stay on the roofs forever. Winter had arrived and it was quickly becoming cold. Yet even with the extra danger, she didn't want to leave Belfast. For the past two years, she'd spent her time in the woods and around small farms. She'd grown tired of stealing eggs from farmers and hunting rabbit and squirrel for dinner.

In Belfast, if you had quick hands and quicker feet, you could steal almost anything; and Alexia had both. If her parents were alive, they wouldn't like the idea of her stealing. But they were not. Besides, she never stole from someone younger than her.

As she squatted on the peaked roof of a bakery, Alexia inhaled the aroma of fresh bread. She'd been eyeing a particularly large loaf that had disappeared into a wood oven. In a few minutes the baker would pull it out and set it up high to cool. If Alexia were quick about it, the baker would never see her. Yet even if he did, the man was far too large and slow to follow her across the rooftops of Belfast.

"I've been watching you."

Alexia started, and almost lost her balance. She turned to see a boy who looked to be two or three years younger, rocking on his heels in the crook of the roof. He had a cheeky grin.

"What do you want?" Alexia growled. She hated being sneaked up on.

"I want to be friends," he said. "I think you need a friend—and I know we do."

Alexia glanced around to see if anyone else was with the boy. "What do you mean *we*?"

"There are a few of us who've decided to stick together," the boy said. "You know, kids like me and you who don't have parents."

"You don't know anything about me!" Alexia said. "I don't need friends!"

"Everyone needs someone," the boy said. "Please, just come and meet the others. I know you'll like us!" He stood and stepped forward, offering a hand. "My name is Josiah, and I want to be your friend."

Alexia shifted warily. *What does he really want? He's probably trying to steal my sling.*

"My name is Blade," Alexia said, "and you had better get away from me. I told you, I don't need friends. Besides, you're just a stupid kid. I wouldn't want to be your friend anyway." Alexia hadn't used her real name since her parents died. She'd chosen Blade because it sounded impressive and dangerous.

A pained look crossed Josiah's face as he backed away. "I just thought maybe …"

Without another word, Alexia leaped past him and sprinted up the roof. She kept running until she was sure Josiah could not possibly have followed.

She was still furious hours later. *How dare he talk about my parents! I should have punched him in the face.* She was perched on the roof of Fibber McGees, a pub that was impressively tall. This was one of her favorite places in all of Belfast. It gave her a good view of the market. Alexia was searching for the best place to steal her dinner when she heard the voice.

"Oi, what's this?" Just below, an older boy with fiery red hair stepped from the shadows. He wasn't talking to Alexia but to someone she couldn't see. "It's a little rat! 'Ello, little rat. What are you doing in my territory, then?"

Josiah stepped from the shadows of a nearby building. *What's he doing here?* Alexia thought crossly.

"I didn't know this was your territory," Josiah said. "Honest to goodness, Petrus, I had no idea!"

So that's Petrus! Alexia had heard about the boy. Everyone said he was cruel and beat up anyone who got in his way. He was the leader of a gang of kids a few years older than Alexia; they were called the Gang of Terror. They were responsible for much of the thievery and pickpocketing in Belfast.

Alexia had heard the Gang of Terror worked for a man who was utterly ruthless. No one knew who he was or what he looked like, but his name was Lord Korah, and the stories she'd heard had given her nightmares.

Besides Josiah and the farmer who tried to kidnap her, Alexia hadn't talked to anyone since her arrival in Belfast. This was normal; she'd barely talked to anyone since her parents died. But Alexia knew how to eavesdrop better than anyone in the city. She would hang unseen from the eaves of the corners of the buildings and hear all sorts of things.

She watched as four more boys appeared from the shadows, sneaking up behind Josiah. As Josiah took a fearful step back, for just a moment he glanced up at Alexia.

He knows I'm here! Alexia was shocked. *He was following me again!* Although she was furious, a part of her was impressed. *The boy has gumption*, she thought. In truth, she didn't know what "gumption" meant, but she'd heard it used before and liked the sound of it.

One of the boys grabbed Josiah from behind and held him tight. "What should we do with the little rat?" Petrus began to laugh. "There are far too many rats in this city nowadays. Maybe we should make an example of this one. If we hurt him, real bad like, maybe it will teach the other rats to stay out of my territory."

"Please don't hurt me," Josiah pleaded. "I didn't know this was your territory!"

"You didn't know?" Petrus extended his arms wide. "All of Belfast is mine."

Alexia decided it was past time she left. What was it to her if the stupid boy was about to get a beating? She didn't care. As she walked up the peak of the roof, she heard the sound of Petrus's fist thud into Josiah's stomach.

The other boys began to laugh as Josiah cried out.

Alexia took another step.

Smack! The sound came again as Josiah whimpered. "Please, Petrus. Don't hit me again. I promise I ..." Alexia turned around and saw Petrus's fist go back again. This time he was going to hit Josiah in the face.

Thwang! The stone crashed into his fist and he shrieked.

Alexia had no doubt she'd broken more than one bone in the bully's hand. "Let him go!" She stood with one foot on the gutter and the other on the shingles. "Let him go or the next one lands between your eyes!"

When Petrus turned his attention on Alexia, her breath caught. The look in his eyes was murder. And at that moment, the gutter gave way.

Thud! Alexia landed flat on her back at Petrus's feet.

Present day

Alexia stood with her back flat against the wall. *The Gang of Terror!* There were seven in all, but Petrus was the worst by far. And he hated Alexia.

What are they doing here? She'd never thought to see them again, but finding them here was crazy.

Petrus closed the door and turned to the others. "Stand up, you louts. We were told to guard the door, not take a nap."

"Shove off!" another boy said. "We've been waiting in this stupid cave all day, and it could be hours yet before they come, if they ever do." The boy had auburn hair and an oafish look. Alexia thought his name was Devin.

Devin closed his eyes and leaned his head against the wall, ignoring the dangerous look in Petrus's eyes. Petrus stepped close and kicked him hard in the ribs. "I told you to get up!" Devin shrieked and scrambled away. "Lord Korah commanded us to stand ready. If you feel like this command is too much for you, I would be happy to let him know."

"All right, all right." Devin raised his hands uneasily. "No need for that. I was only joking!"

Terror formed in the pit of Alexia's stomach as she made her way past the Gang of Terror. *Lord Korah is here!* The thought made her want to scream. Tears formed in her eyes, and as she passed farther out of earshot, she began to run. She needed to catch the men who had taken Wild. If she didn't rescue him before he was taken to Korah, Alexia had no doubt she would never see him again.

Chapter 7

ONE MOUSE AND ONE HUNDRED MONSTER CATS

King Edward and Jack stood at the entrance of a secret passageway at the back of the war chamber. "Few know of these passages," the king said. "They run through the entire palace and were built as an escape route for the royal family. We will use them to take you to the World Portal." Without another word, the king grabbed a lantern from the wall and walked in.

"Your Majesty, how did you know I was going to the World Portal?" Jack asked as they walked through the cramped passageway.

"I have been working with Andreal and Miel," the king said. "But if we are under attack, someone must have betrayed us. As far as I know, only myself, Andreal, and Miel knew the plan to sneak you to the portal." The king shook his head sadly. "If I had to guess, I would say it was Andreal. I have never fully trusted that giant, yet Elion assured me he was true. And who am I to argue with a Sephari?" The ceiling was so low that the king had to hunch as he walked.

"What do you mean—sneak us in?" Jack asked. "You are the king. Couldn't you have just invited us?"

"I could have," King Edward agreed, "but then the world would have known exactly where you were and how you were leaving. We wanted it to be kept secret, though I suppose our planning was for nothing if Andreal was working against us all along."

Jack and the king had arrived at a dead end. The king reached up and pushed on a stone above his head. As the stone disappeared, the wall slid aside to reveal a thin metal slide that dropped into darkness. "This has always been my favorite part!" The king chuckled as he sat down and shoved off.

Jack quickly sat and pushed off behind him. The ride was spectacular! The slide twisted and turned, then dropped suddenly only to twist again. By the time he reached the bottom, he was grinning from ear to ear.

The king was already standing, and when Jack arrived, his smile quickly faded. The muted sounds of battle could be heard on the other side of the thick walls.

"If the fighting has come this far into the palace, we haven't much time," the king said. "And I am afraid I cannot take you any farther, my dear boy." He knelt and lifted a small steel grate from the floor.

"You will need to go the rest of the way on your own. We are only one level above the chamber that holds the World Portal. You will crawl past two metal grates, and when you reach the third, you will be directly above the portal. From there all you need do is remove the grate and drop to the chamber below. The Author willing, Mrs. Dumphry and the others will be waiting!"

"You can't come with me?" Jack pleaded.

"It has been many years since I could fit through a tunnel this small." The king chuckled. "No, I'm afraid I cannot go any farther. But I will join the battle elsewhere and try to buy you and your friends as much time as I can."

An explosion sounded from the other side of the wall. A few small stones fell and dust streamed down. "We haven't much time," the king said. "And though I am enjoying our conversation immensely, I am afraid you must go now."

Jack lowered himself into the tunnel. It was so small he would have to wriggle through on his belly. He met the king's eyes one last time. "Thank you, Your Majesty."

"No, my dear boy, it is I who must thank you. The Awakened stand with you, Jack Staples. And though you carry the weight of the world on your shoulders, we will carry you on ours! Now," he said in a commanding voice, "it is time for you to go. Good-bye, young man. If the Author wills it, we will meet again."

Jack took the king's hand and shook it firmly, then dropped to his belly and began shimmying through the tunnel. "Remember," the king called from behind him, "you must pass the first two metal grates, and when you come to the third, you'll have arrived at the World Portal."

Jack's mind turned somersaults as he squirmed through the tunnel. He'd just met the king of England! As he arrived at the first grate, he heard voices in the cavern below. When he peered through, he saw a young man with red hair sitting on the ground, leaning heavily against the wall.

"I told you to get up!" A black-haired youth appeared, kicking the red-haired boy in the ribs. "Lord Korah commanded us to stand ready. If you feel like this command is too much for you, I would be happy to let him know!"

The first boy leaped out of Jack's view. "All right, all right," he said. "No need for that. I was only joking!" Jack didn't wait to see more. Whoever these boys were, he had no desire to meet them.

A minute later Jack came to the second grate and his breath caught. At least one hundred Oriax were packed into the small room. The beasts were eerily silent, standing perfectly still; every Oriax had its eyes trained on a brick wall.

Whatever was happening, Jack wanted to be as far away from this chamber as possible. He hadn't wanted to think about what would happen if he arrived at the third chamber and none of his friends were there. Would he leave without them? Would he even know how?

Arthur Greaves was scared witless. He stood in a small chamber surrounded by thirty-five Oriax. He was trapped as sure as a fly in honey. Without Jack's Atherial Cloak, he'd have become Oriax food long ago.

When Jack fled the courtyard an hour earlier, Arthur had tried to follow. His best friend had disappeared through a ruined door in the side of the palace, but Arthur needed to sneak around a number of Oriax first. By the time he entered the palace, Jack was gone, though Arthur had found his leather satchel lying among the rubble. He'd been astounded to find the Atherial Cloak inside. Arthur decided to wear the cloak until he could return it, but he hadn't been able to find Jack. Instead, he'd managed to find a large number of Oriax.

Skulking through the endless corridors, Arthur had quickly become lost. When he happened upon a large stairwell, he remembered Mrs. Dumphry saying something about the World Portal being below the dungeons. *If I keep going down*, he thought, *I'll have to find them eventually.*

After descending thirty-five flights of stairs, Arthur was regretting his decision very much. At the bottom, he'd been shocked to find ten Oriax sitting quietly in a small chamber, staring at a brick wall. He quickly began the endless climb back to the top. But before he'd gone five steps, eighteen more Oriax appeared on the stairs above. They walked, slithered, hopped, and crawled in absolute silence and entered the small chamber to sit beside the others and stare at the brick wall.

It was an eerie situation, and Arthur could see no chance of escape. He stood with his back flat against the wall and tried not to breathe. He knew the cloak didn't render him totally invisible and was afraid to move a muscle. If the Oriax hadn't been staring so intently at the wall, he was sure at least one of the beasts would have seen him by now.

No! His heart sank yet again. Another thirty Oriax descended the stairs, pushing their way into the chamber. Arthur quickly realized there wasn't enough space for all of the beasts. When even more Oriax appeared in the stairwell, he dropped to his belly and rolled beneath the haunches of one of the beasts just before it bumped into him.

Back in Ballylesson, Arthur had once seen two cats playing with a mouse. The cats had faced each other and let the mouse run back and forth between them. Each time the poor rodent tried to escape, one of the cats would swat it toward the other, which would chomp down on the mouse's tail and toss it high into the air. The poor mouse would land, then frantically try to scurry away, but the other cat would swat it aside once again. The poor thing never had a chance.

Arthur lay flat on his back, staring up at an Oriax with the body of a bear and the head and shoulders of a horse. He couldn't get the image of the mouse out of his mind. The horrid cats had tossed the poor thing between them for twenty minutes before growing tired of the game. And then, seeming almost bored, one cat had snapped the head off the mouse and left the rest to the second cat.

Arthur wanted to scream as even more Oriax entered the chamber. *What are they doing here?* And that's when he heard it. Something else was descending the stairs. A low scraping echoed from the stairwell, and as the noise grew, every Oriax turned its head in anticipation. The beasts began shoving against one another to clear a path to the back of the chamber as Arthur shimmied beneath them.

All Arthur could see were two silvery, clawed feet that looked to be a mixture of human and animal. The creature stepped into the chamber and inhaled deeply, then began walking toward the back wall. Just as it was about to pass Arthur, it stopped and inhaled again.

"There is something … wrong here," it purred. "A Light Eyes is here; I can smell it."

Every Oriax began to snarl in agitation.

"Show yourself, Light Eyes," the creature hissed.

Arthur froze. *No!* He hadn't thought it possible to be any more afraid, but he'd been wrong. *It can smell me!* The thought paralyzed him.

"Rise. Rise and face me." The Oriax snarls grew louder.

Arthur didn't move. He squeezed his eyes shut and tried desperately to summon lightning, but nothing happened.

"RISE!" The creature raged and the torches dimmed slightly.

And Arthur stood. There was nothing else he could think to do. He shoved his way between two Oriax and stood shoulder to shoulder with the beasts. Ever so slowly, he opened the Atherial Cloak and pulled back the hood. The Oriax went crazy, snapping jaws, growling, howling, and hissing. But they did not attack.

The creature seemed curious as it looked at Arthur. "I have heard of you, Lightning Dancer." It purred as it made a half bow and gave a flourish of its silvery cloak. "I am pleased to meet you. You are a friend to the Children of Prophecy, are you not?"

Lightning Dancer? It knows me! Arthur hadn't thought the dark servants knew anything about him, but this creature knew something Arthur had only just learned.

Where there should have been eyes, the creature had large, oval mirrors, and its ears were pointed at the bottom. Its skin was pure silver, and its face had a feline quality.

"What ..." Arthur gulped. "What are you going to do to me?"

The creature smiled as it began to contort, folding inward. "First," it said, "I will become you."

Arthur gasped. He was now standing before the mirror image of himself! The creature that looked like Arthur smiled and spoke in Arthur's own voice. "I am a Grendall, of course. And I will do what I do best. I will draw close to your friends, and I will kill them one by one." The Grendall licked its lips.

Arthur tried to step back, but an Oriax with the head of a hyena and the body of a walrus snapped at him.

"As for what we will do with you," the Grendall said, "that is not my decision. I must consult the master."

Arthur shuddered. The creature still looked like him, except that its eyes had once again become large mirrors. They didn't reflect the chamber, but showed another place. After a moment, a man with jet-black hair and wearing a black-and-silver cloak appeared in the creature's mirrored eyes. Although Arthur didn't understand it, he guessed the eyes acted as some sort of two-way mirror.

"Are you in place?"

"Yes, Master Korah." The Grendall spoke in its purring voice. "We await your signal."

"We leave now. Kill anyone who tries to enter the chamber."

"Yes, master," the Grendall hissed. "As you can see, I have captured the Lightning Dancer. What would you have me do with him?"

"We have no use for the fat one." Korah sounded bored. "You can kill him now."

"It will be as you command." The mirrors in the other Arthur's eyes faded.

"It has been far too long since I have consumed a Light Eyes." The Grendall smacked its lips in anticipation. "And I am hungry."

Chapter 8

HELLO, FATHER

Six years, two months, and fourteen days earlier

Bruises covered Alexia's body. Her hands were tied behind her back and every muscle burned. Petrus had been furious with Alexia for breaking his hand, and his Gang of Terror had punched and kicked her repeatedly until she'd fallen unconscious.

Alexia opened her eyes and groaned as she rolled onto her side. She was laying face-first and was sure at least two of her ribs were cracked.

No! Where are they? Alexia's dress and sling were gone, and she wore only her shift. The thought was almost too much to bear.

For the first time since she'd been captured, Alexia allowed herself to cry.

Alexia heard someone groan behind her. She rolled over and saw Josiah lying on his back. He had also been beaten. *I should have left him there!* she thought for the twentieth time since the fall.

Yet she knew it wasn't true. It had been the right thing to help Josiah. In truth, she was furious with herself. Stepping on a gutter and losing her balance was such a stupid thing to do. Josiah groaned again.

"Boy," Alexia whispered. "Boy, I'm here. Are you okay?"

He opened his eyes and smiled weakly. "Thanks"—he licked his lips—"for coming back for me."

Alexia let out a small sigh. "You're welcome. Though I didn't do such a great job at rescuing you."

"You tried," he said. "That's all that matters."

"I may have made things worse, breaking Petrus's hand like that."

Josiah grinned. "Yeah, but did you see his face?"

Petrus had looked ridiculous, jumping up and down, screaming like a baby. Alexia giggled, then immediately regretted it when the pain in her ribs stabbed her. "We need to get out of here," she whispered. "I don't think they'll ever let us go after what I did."

"It's not Petrus I'm afraid of," Josiah said. "It's their leader, Lord Korah. He doesn't just hurt people. He's killed people, lots of them."

Alexia had also heard the stories, though no one knew for certain if this Lord Korah was even real. He was said to be the mastermind behind the Gang of Terror and other gangs in Belfast. But she didn't care how terrible he was. All she cared about was getting her sling and dress back.

Her wrists had been tied tight with ropes, and she didn't think she could wriggle out of them. Alexia rolled away again. There were a few stones lying about, but nothing looked sharp enough to cut the rope that bound her.

"Do you mind if I untie you?"

Alexia rolled to her back and was shocked to see Josiah standing above her, his hands free. He was grinning sheepishly.

"How did you ... what did ...?"

"I've always been good at getting out of things. I think it helps that I can do this." Josiah twisted his arms in on themselves—he was double-jointed at the wrists and elbows.

Alexia grinned. "Why didn't you say so, you ninny! Yes, untie me!"

Josiah snickered as he fiddled with the knot. Alexia stood and rubbed her wrists, looking around. They weren't in a locked room but had been left in some sort of tunnel.

"This must be a part of their lair," she said.

"Yeah, but which way will take us out of here?"

"I'm not going anywhere until I get my dress and sling back," she said bitterly. "Petrus stole them!"

"You can get another dress and sling." Josiah was incredulous. "Let's just get out of here!"

Alexia rounded on him. "Go if you want, boy. I never asked for your help. But I'm not leaving without them."

Josiah threw his hands in the air. "I didn't say I wouldn't help. If it's that important to you, then of course I'll help. Why do you have to be so prickly all the time?"

Alexia was confused. What did this boy really want? After a moment she realized she didn't care. It would be nice to have someone nearby if she really was going to search for Petrus. "Fine," she said. "You can come. But you had better not slow me down."

Josiah grinned, rocking on his heels and looking as if he were about to embark on a grand adventure. Alexia rolled her eyes as she studied the tunnel, looking for any clue as to which way to go. When she found none, she decided to pick a direction and start walking. As they crept along the tunnel, Josiah whispered, "Is your name really Blade?"

"Yes," Alexia said. "Why? What's wrong with it?"

"I can't imagine a better name. I wish my name was Blade."

Alexia was beginning to like this boy. They hadn't gone far before they heard screams. Someone was in trouble! They shared an uneasy look as they continued forward.

"Please stop! Please," a boy shrieked, "I beg you!"

"I warned you what would happen if you failed me!" a man snarled.

"Please …"

Alexia and Josiah rounded a corner and stopped. They'd come to a section where six passages joined, forming a large chamber. A man in a black-and-silver hooded cloak held a leather strap and stood over Petrus, who lay whimpering on the ground.

A few older boys and girls stood nearby, looking as if they would rather be anywhere else. If Alexia had to guess, these were the members of the Gang of Terror. Which meant the man must be Lord Korah. *I bet that's why they left us alone,* Alexia thought. *They're all here to watch Petrus get punished.*

Alexia disliked Petrus; in fact, she hated him. But a small part of her felt bad for him. What had he done to make Korah so angry? The man's face was shrouded in the deep hood, but there was something familiar about him.

"You are meant to bring this city to its knees," Korah said. "You are to steal from everyone, rich and poor, to destroy property. You are to hurt those who are weaker and humiliate those who are stronger. Yet you allow a little girl to break your hand?" He sighed. "You are weak, boy! Perhaps I was mistaken to place you in command here?"

"She ambushed us, m'lord!" Petrus sniveled.

"You were ambushed by a little girl?" Korah sneered. "Pathetic!"

Alexia couldn't believe what she was hearing. *Petrus is being punished because I broke his hand? Josiah is right—Korah is evil!*

"I am not known for giving second chances"—Korah shook his head disgustedly—"but I'm feeling ... gracious today. You will remain the leader here, but I warn you, do not fail me again." His voice was as cold as the grave.

Korah had been pacing, but he stopped suddenly. "What is that?"

Alexia couldn't see what he was looking at.

Petrus groaned and held his ribs as he stood. "Just the girl's things, m'lord—a dress and sling. Nothing important." Alexia's heart leaped—then sank. She'd found them, but now what?

"Give them to me." Korah's voice was tight.

Petrus scrambled over and handed them to Korah. He hissed the moment his fingers touched the dress. After a moment he began inspecting it, looking closely at the seams and running his fingers along the material. "I don't believe it," he whispered. "Could it be? After so long, to find her here?"

"I'm sorry, m'lord, are you speaking to me?" Petrus asked.

Korah ignored Petrus as he moved on to inspect the sling. After a moment he brought both sling and dress to his nose and inhaled deeply. After a moment, he screamed and tore Alexia's dress, ripping it in two. But he didn't stop there—he tore it over and over again until it was shredded beyond recognition. Alexia gasped, but Josiah grabbed her and placed a hand over her mouth to keep her from screaming.

Alexia shoved Josiah off and glared at him. But she stayed put. Although she hated to admit it, he was right. To attack now would only ensure they were captured again.

"Take me to her!" Korah raged. "This child escaped me once. Tonight I will finish what was started years ago!" He turned to the others. "Come with me and I will teach you how to make someone truly suffer."

"Yes, m'lord." Petrus whimpered and darted toward the tunnel where Alexia and Josiah were hiding. Both children scrambled into one of the side tunnels, doing their best to stay hidden in the shadows. Korah dropped the sling and the ruined dress as he followed Petrus and the others out of the chamber. As he stalked past, Alexia once again had the nagging feeling that she knew the man from somewhere. *And he acted like he knew me!* It didn't make a lick of sense. As they darted across the chamber to snatch the sling and shredded dress, Alexia began to weep. Her dress was ruined. It had been a present from her mother and now it was gone.

Present day

As Alexia crept along the dark caverns below Buckingham Palace, she took a stone from the inside pocket of her crimson cloak and dropped it into the fold of her sling. She still wore the Atherial Cloak and was sure the captain and his men had no idea she was following.

They were far enough from the Gang of Terror for Alexia to try to save Wild without being heard. She had to do it before he was taken to Korah. Whatever happened, she could not allow that! As she spun the sling, the captain stopped abruptly and knocked on a large steel door.

The door swung open and Alexia almost gasped when she saw Miel standing on the other side. Alexia had barely spoken to her in Agartha, but she had liked the woman. Could Miel be the betrayer Mrs. Dumphry had spoken of?

"Who is it now?" a harsh voice growled from somewhere inside the chamber.

Alexia felt something cold wrap around her heart. She recognized that voice from when she'd heard it in the tunnels more than six years earlier. Korah was on the other side of the steel door.

Miel looked from the captain to Wild. "They have brought the old woman's pup. The boy, Wild."

"Excellent," Korah said. "Bring him to me."

As the men carried Wild into the chamber, Alexia took a deep breath. It was too late to turn back now. She slung a stone against a nearby wall, and as Miel turned to look, Alexia darted through the door. Though her trick had worked on Petrus, as she passed Miel, the woman looked directly at her and gasped. "The witch has come!"

Alexia sent a stone flying at Miel, but the woman dove aside and it passed through empty space. The two frightened guards dropped Wild and scrambled out of the chamber with the captain.

As Alexia readied another stone, Wild rose from the ground and spun. In a heartbeat he'd reached inside his cloak and sent two daggers flying at Miel's chest.

He must have been conscious the whole time! Alexia was outraged. *He wanted to be brought here!* If she'd known he was awake, she could have rescued him earlier!

The Atherial Cloak was affecting Alexia's aim, so she shrugged out of it. As she loosed another stone, Korah extended his arms and sent a wall of black flame exploding across the chamber. Alexia somersaulted out of its path, and as she landed, both Korah and Alexia saw each other clearly for the first time. He was standing in front of a massive structure of interlocking steel rings.

"It's not Elion!" Korah whispered hoarsely. "It's the Child of Prophecy!"

"She wears the witch's cloak." Miel was just as shaken as Korah. Wild lay on the ground nearby, groaning and cradling a wounded arm.

"It's you!" Alexia croaked, suddenly unable to fill her lungs. She couldn't stop the tears as she stepped back. "I don't understand …"

Wild somehow managed to rise and leap at Korah. "Leave her alone!" he screamed.

Korah didn't even glance at him but pointed a finger and sent a stream of black flame to explode against Wild's chest. Wild shot backward, crashed against the wall, and fell.

Alexia tried to breathe, but she couldn't find air. Her chest felt tight as she crumpled to her knees. "Father?" Tears streamed from her eyes as she tried to make sense of what she was seeing. "Father,

I don't understand! What's happening?" Standing next to the steel rings was Alexia's father. Her father was Lord Korah.

Just before she fainted, Alexia saw her father and Miel share a confused look. From somewhere outside the chamber, multiple explosions sounded, but Alexia barely heard them.

Chapter 9

THROUGH THE PORTAL

Jack crawled through the tunnel and quickly approached the third grate. Someone was arguing in the chamber that held the World Portal! He peered through the grate. Directly below was a large structure of interlocking steel rings forming the shape of a ball. He had seen the exact same structure in the Council Chamber in Agartha, though it had been damaged when the city fell.

Standing beside the rings was a man in a black-and-silver cloak. "That has to be it," a woman's voice came from somewhere below. "There's no other explanation!" Jack tried to get a better look but couldn't see her.

"Impossible," the man said. "She looks nothing like them!"

"Think, Korah!" the woman said. "Why else would she believe it? She may not be their daughter, but they raised her! The witch and the Staples woman must have switched the children just after they were born. You must remember that night! We thought we misread the stars, but the Child of Prophecy had been born!"

Jack's breath caught; they were talking about his mother! Korah was silent a moment, then sighed. "If you're right, then we let the Child of Prophecy slip through our fingers."

As the woman stepped into view, Jack suppressed a gasp. *Miel!* The woman sat on the Council of Seven and had fought to defend Agartha.

"Maybe the witch helped her escape, or maybe the child was lucky," Miel said, "but it's the only thing that makes sense. But you are missing the point! We can use this. If the girl truly believes it, she'll do anything you ask!"

A chime sounded from somewhere, and the air in front of Korah rippled. Jack's jaw dropped as dark mist appeared and formed into a mirror floating in midair. In the mirror was a silvery creature with a catlike face. It had mirrors for eyes, and its ears were pointed at the bottom.

"Are you in place?" Korah said to the creature.

"Yes, Master Korah," it purred. "We await your signal."

"We leave now. Kill anyone who tries to enter the chamber."

"Yes, Lord Korah," the silvery creature hissed. "As you can see, I have captured the Lightning Dancer. What would you have me do with him?"

The mirror blurred for a moment, and when it became clear again, Jack saw Arthur. He was standing in a small chamber, surrounded by at least a hundred Oriax. *He must be in the chamber directly behind me!*

"We have no use for the fat one," Korah said. "You can kill him now."

"It will be as you command," the creature purred. As the mirror of mist dissipated, the silvery creature smacked its lips in anticipation.

Panic rose inside Jack. He had to save Arthur! As he struggled to crawl backward through the tunnel, Jack saw Korah step toward the World Portal and place his hands on the rings. "Thaltorose!" he snarled, and the rings began to vibrate.

Jack didn't wait to see what happened. He needed to save his best friend.

Arthur stood in the center of a cramped cavern surrounded by a hundred Oriax. Though he was terrified, something else was happening inside him. He understood he was about to die, and more than anything—even more than saving his life—he wanted to stop the Grendall.

"First, I will become you," the creature had said. "Then I will kill your friends, one by one." It made Arthur furious to think of this creature attacking Jack and the others while looking and sounding like Arthur Greaves. *I'm sorry, Jack!*

The Grendall licked its lips as it approached. The Oriax growled in anticipation but did not attack. Their eyes were glued to the

Grendall. Arthur tried to imagine lightning raining down, but nothing happened. He tried to "feel the electricity," as Mrs. Dumphry had told him to do, but all he felt was fear.

"What do ye think yer doin', ye mangy feline?" a rumbling voice called from the stairwell. Arthur turned to see Andreal standing at the bottom of the stairs. He was so tall his fire-red hair brushed the cavern ceiling. The giant held a wicked, half-mooned ax in each hand, and his black beard glistened as if soaked in oil. Andreal stepped forward and in one giant leap spun and struck out with both blades. As he landed next to Arthur, five Oriax lay dead around them.

The giant wore a thick black kilt and leather-studded jerkin and had a crazed look in his eyes. The Grendall hissed warily. The Oriax snarled and gurgled their nervous displeasure but did nothing.

"I hope ye no mind me joining ye," Andreal said to Arthur. "I know ye be having it under control, but I couldn't let ye have all the fun!"

Arthur stared at the giant, unable to think how to respond. Andreal chuckled merrily, then turned his gaze to the Grendall. "Ye should have killed me yerself, ye filthy mongrel. The hundred or so beasts ye sent are dead. So I'll be giving ye one chance to tell me! Where be the traitor? Where be Miel?"

Before the creature could respond, a loud thrumming echoed through the chamber as the ground trembled and dust rained down. "You are too late, giant!" The Grendall darted to the back wall, placed its palms flat against the stone, and pushed. Arthur gasped as the wall began to disintegrate.

"We be almost out of time!" Andreal rumbled above the loud thrumming. "The World Portal be opening." Andreal placed both axes in one hand and grabbed Arthur by the back of the neck. "The only way to kill a Grendall be to take out one of its eyes," he said. "But make sure ye pick the right one or ye'll just make it angry!"

Why is he telling me this? Arthur wondered. *Surely he doesn't think I will* … Without warning the giant threw the Atherial Cloak hood over Arthur's head and catapulted him over the Oriax and in the direction of the Grendall.

Arthur hit the ground and skidded to a stop only a few paces behind the creature that still looked like him. As he scrambled to his feet, he glanced back to see Andreal clang his axes together and scream, "Now, let's dance, ye filthy mutts!" As one, the Oriax swarmed over the giant like a hive of raging bees.

As the Grendall lowered its arms, the wall that had been at the back of the chamber was gone and only a small pile of dust remained. On the other side of the ruined wall a fierce battle raged.

Jack's jaw dropped. Andreal was just below, laughing like a madman. The giant spun and leaped among a massive number of Oriax, thrusting his two axes in a dizzying fury. The half-moon blades cleaved a bloody path through the attacking beasts.

As he pulled the grate aside, Jack felt a small pang of guilt for thinking Andreal had been a traitor. He lowered his head through the opening and could barely believe his eyes.

Aias fought a Shadule in a deadly duel. Each time their blades met, gold and black lightning splintered the air. Behind Aias, Elion battled against impossible odds. She leaped between the second Shadule and at least twenty Oriax, swinging her short sword with dizzying speed. Her eyes and hair blazed and gravity meant nothing to her. She leaped from wall to ceiling to floor effortlessly, and where her feet trod, colored mist filled the chamber with unearthly light.

When Jack spotted Arthur, he blinked. There were two Arthurs, and they were fighting each other, rolling across the floor. He was so stunned he almost lost his grip. Arthur Greaves fought against … Arthur Greaves!

Both Arthurs choked and clawed at each other—and Jack was sure that if he didn't act soon, one of the Arthurs was going to die. He tried not to think as he lowered himself to the chamber below.

Fierce fighting raged all around, yet every man, beast, and creature was so intent on the attack that none noticed the boy who appeared among them. Jack moved like a mouse, darting across the chamber toward the fighting Arthurs. As he approached, he drew Ashandar. Even with his recent training, the black blade still felt clumsy in his hands.

Jack had never been able to repeat what happened on the streets of Ballylesson when the sword had taken on a life of its own. Mrs. Dumphry claimed the blade was both weapon and teacher; that the more Jack surrendered to it, the more he would learn. But Jack hadn't been able to figure out how to surrender to a piece of metal.

"Get off him!" Jack pointed Ashandar at both of the Arthurs. One of the Arthurs was choking the other, who had turned a silvery shade of gray. When the attacking Arthur looked at him, he leaped back and raised his hands.

"Jack!" the attacking Arthur yelled. "You're alive! You have no idea how glad I am to see you!" He glanced at the second Arthur. "That's not me; it's a monster and it was going to kill you. It's called a Grendall," Arthur said. "It made itself look like me, somehow. Except it's not me, obviously, because I am me. We have to kill it, Jack!"

Jack blinked. It sure sounded like Arthur. Whenever his best friend got excited, he talked so fast it was impossible to get a word in.

The second Arthur was still down. "He's lying, Jack!" the second Arthur screamed. "You have to believe me!"

Jack shifted his blade between the two Arthurs. "Where did I first meet you?"

The second Arthur paled and screamed, "We don't have time, Jack! You have to kill him before it's too late!"

The first Arthur smiled. "We were in a mud puddle outside the schoolhouse. Jonty Dobson threw us both in there!"

The second Arthur hissed and transformed into the silvery creature Jack had seen in the mirror of mist. Jack raised Ashandar high as the Grendall let out a rictus snarl. It moved like a cat, circling the boys.

"I will consume you both!" it purred, crouching low.

"Grendall!" Mrs. Dumphry shouted.

Jack turned to see his ancient teacher standing with arms outstretched. The Grendall stood up and hissed angrily. "You have lost, ancient one," it cried. "My master has the child!"

Mrs. Dumphry stepped forward and released a ball of flames. But the Grendall was quick—it scurried into the shadows, meowing like a sick cat.

Mrs. Dumphry didn't pursue. She leaned heavily against the back wall, and when she met Jack's eyes, she spoke in a strangled voice.

"They have taken Alexia! They have kidnapped the Child of Prophecy!"

Chapter 10

THALTOROSE

Alexia ran through a field of bloodred flowers. The sun shone brightly overhead, and she felt … happy. It had been many years since she'd been truly happy—not since the day of her fifth birthday.

She slowed at the thought. "What happened on my fifth birthday?" she wondered aloud. For a moment, she felt a stabbing in her heart, but just as quickly, the pain was gone. She darted forward again, laughing as she ran.

I'm going to pick some flowers for Mother. I just know she'll give me a big hug when I bring them home! Once again, the thought of her mother brought a sharp stab to Alexia's heart. Pushing it aside, she slowed and began collecting the most beautiful red wildflowers she'd ever seen. Laughing aloud, she grabbed armfuls of them, so many she was barely able to hold them all.

Mother will be so surprised. Why did the thought of her mother make her feel sad? For some reason, Alexia couldn't make her mind stand still.

Alexia suddenly realized she had no idea where she was. As she turned to look, her jaw dropped. In the valley below was an arena of sleek black stone that stood as tall as a mountain. As she looked at the arena, panic rose inside her. She felt it calling to her, willing her to come.

"I need to find Mother and Father," she whispered. "I need to tell them about the ..."

Fire.

Alexia dropped her armful of flowers. Why couldn't she remember? Something bad had happened. She placed her hands on her head.

Raging fire.

Dropping to her knees, Alexia was unable to breathe.

"NO!" she screamed. In the ground in front of her were three freshly dug graves.

"Father!" Alexia bolted up. She was sitting in a bed in a darkened room.

It took a moment to realize she'd been dreaming. It was a dream she'd had many times since her fifth birthday, and every time she woke, she experienced the heartache all over again. Yet this time when she awoke, she heard the voice of her father.

"Alexia, I am here. You are safe now." He patted her on the head.

Alexia froze. She remembered everything. Her father was alive. Her father was Korah. And suddenly everything seemed wrong with the world.

"What's happening?" Her voice trembled. "I don't understand ..."

Her father lit a lamp. And when he turned to her, he smiled stiffly. "We have much to catch up on," he said. "And I promise we will talk soon. But first I must introduce you to someone."

Alexia tried to calm herself as her father walked to the door. She couldn't believe he was alive! *Alive!* The thought was almost too much to bear. She wanted to run over and throw her arms around him. But it didn't make sense! How could her father possibly be Lord Korah?

She shivered as she scanned the bedchamber. The bed was far bigger than most beds, and the walls were encrusted with diamonds and other gemstones. The floor was rich marble, the ceiling pure gold. But rather than beautiful, the room seemed somehow ... wrong. It was as if the jewels and gold were covering something dark and sinister. The shadows at the periphery of Alexia's vision were darker than they should have been; they almost seemed to be moving.

Her father opened the door. "He is my lord and master and the father of all. You have called him Assassin, but I call him King." Korah bowed low, but Alexia began to whimper. Standing in the entry was a man in a white cloak. Darkness radiated from him, and his skin sparkled like diamonds. He was covered in a thin layer of sweat, and each fingernail was overly long and lacquered in multiple colors. In place of his eyes were endless caverns of fire.

"Hello, Alexia." The Assassin's voice was jarring, like two forms of music clashing. "I have been wanting to meet you for a very long time."

Alexia hadn't realized she'd been moving until she felt the wall against her back. "Father, no!" she shouted. "He's the one who sent the Shadule! He is the reason our house was burned and you and Mother died … or"—she glanced at her father—"at least, the reason Mother died!" She was shaking. The Assassin now stood directly in front of her, and her father merely watched.

"Alexia," her father said, "the old woman and the witch have been lying to you. They are the ones who burned our house that day. They are the ones who killed your mother."

She shook her head. "No! Father, it's not true! You must believe me! When I fought the Shadule in Agartha, it told me it killed you. It told me it burned our house!"

"And yet here I am, alive and well." Her father held out his hands as if in proof. "The Shadule are simple creatures and often struggle with our language. I am here right now and I am telling you it was Mrs. Dumphry and Elion who killed your mother. They tried to kill me as well, but I escaped. I've spent these last years doing nothing but search for you."

"My lady," the Assassin said in the voice of a freshly dug grave, "you must know that you are special. I have not brought you here to hurt you, but to give you the honor you deserve. You will never have to run again. You will never need to humble yourself before anyone. My darling Alexia"—the Assassin's smile didn't reach his flaming eyes—"you have finally come home." He held out a hand. "Come, and I will show you the greatest city in the world."

Alexia couldn't stop shaking. She wanted to retch at the sickly sweet smell that engulfed him. She shook her head but couldn't find a coherent thought. But when she looked at her father, he nodded encouragingly.

"My lady, I want to show you the city because it is my gift to you," the Assassin said. "Everything I have is yours. Every gemstone in this city belongs to you. Every slave will live or die at your command."

Alexia's father smiled as she took hold of the Assassin's hand. Something inside her screamed that it was wrong, but she shoved the feeling down. There was a small part of her that didn't care. She was with her father, and she was so tired of running. As the Assassin's hand wrapped around hers, the putrid smell made it hard to breathe.

The Assassin escorted her to the balcony, where he threw back the curtains. When she saw the city, Alexia started to scream—it was more evil than anything she could have imagined. Everywhere she looked were monsters and horrors beyond belief; it was a city of shadows and nightmares. Alexia felt the world slip away as she fainted at the Assassin's feet.

The fighting was over. The small band of Awakened still lived, though all were injured and in low spirits, in spite of the fact that Aias and Elion had managed to dispatch two Shadule. Alexia had been taken, and no one had seen Wild since the battle started in the courtyard.

They had entered the chamber that housed the World Portal and locked the door tight. Jack, Arthur, Aias, and Mrs. Dumphry sat facing one another as Elion stood nearby, staring at the unmoving steel rings. Andreal lay on the cold stone floor, snoring loudly.

"You're sure he said Thaltorose?" Aias demanded again. "Please, Jack, you must be sure!"

"Yes," Jack said. "He placed his hands on the rings and said 'Thaltorose' loudly. What does it mean?"

Mrs. Dumphry and Aias shared a knowing look. "Thaltorose is also known as the City of Shadows," Mrs. Dumphry said. "It is where the Assassin first earned his name and the Shadowfog was birthed. But most importantly, it is where the Assassin now lives and is raising an army. If Alexia has been taken to Thaltorose"—she let out a tired breath—"getting her back will be next to impossible."

"But we can't just leave her," Arthur said. "She's one of us!"

"Child, I did not say we would leave her. I said it would be next to impossible to rescue her," Mrs. Dumphry snapped. "Of course we must try." She turned her gaze on Jack. "But we cannot allow the Assassin to have both children."

"I fear we have no choice but to split up," Elion said as she turned from the rings. "We need the wisdom of Time, now more than ever. I will take Jack to the Forbidden Garden while the rest of you travel to Thaltorose to rescue Alexia."

"Are ye sure ye don't need at least one ax by yer side?" Andreal asked. He'd awoken and was rubbing his hands vigorously over his face.

"I am not sure of anything," Elion said. "And I fear Mrs. Dumphry is right; you are most likely marching to your deaths. But we cannot abandon Alexia to the Assassin. You have no choice but to enter the City of Shadows."

"Should we no' try to raise an army," Andreal asked, "so we can be attacking the city in force?"

"A small band may be better than an army," Elion said, "and we cannot wait. We must not delay even an hour. The World Portal will not take you all the way to the City of Shadows. The land surrounding the city has been corrupted, and though you could travel out by way of the World Portal, you cannot travel in. If you are lucky, you will arrive ten or twelve days out from the city. If you few can get into the city without being seen, perhaps you can rescue Alexia before the Assassin knows you're there." She turned her gaze on Aias and Mrs. Dumphry. "The two of you know the city more than anyone, and that may be the advantage we need."

Jack was on the verge of tears. Thinking of Alexia in the hands of the Assassin was almost too much to bear.

Elion looked from Jack to Arthur. "It is time to say your good-byes. The Author willing, we will all meet again. But we must not delay."

Jack jumped up. "You can't mean to send Arthur with them!"

Elion smiled sadly. "Only you will enter the Forbidden Garden, Jack. It would be too dangerous to try and send Arthur in with you." Her eyes blazed with a golden light as she turned to Arthur. "Though you are young, Arthur Greaves, you are powerful and courageous. And something tells me that if this mission has any chance of success, it will be because you were there. I will not make you go, but I am asking you. Will you join Mrs. Dumphry and the others?"

"No!" Tears stung Jack's eyes as he turned to Arthur. "You can't leave me!"

Arthur stood, and he didn't seem afraid. A look of resolve had entered his eyes. "You are my best friend," Arthur said. "And I don't know what I'll do without you. But if my going gives Alexia a better chance, how can I say no?"

Jack didn't know what to say. Arthur wrapped him in a fierce hug. "You have something you must do, and now, so do I. I'm going to miss you!" he whispered.

"We will see each other again," Jack whispered back. "We have to. Don't go getting yourself killed or anything stupid like that!"

Arthur slapped his forehead. "I almost forgot!" He fished in his coat and pulled out the Atherial Cloak. "You dropped this earlier and I saved it for you."

"You keep it," Jack said. "You'll need it more than I."

"No! It's yours. Elion gave it to you."

"Then it's mine to do with as I please." Jack glanced at Elion, who nodded. "Besides," he said, "I'm not giving it to you. I'm just lending it until we see each other again."

"It is time, Jack." Elion stood next to the World Portal. The seven rings that had been standing still were now spinning rapidly as silver light spilled out, bathing the chamber in its glow. A loud thrumming sound bounced around them.

Jack wrapped Arthur in another hug, then wiped his tears as he joined Elion. She grabbed his hand and whispered, "Don't be afraid. Breathe deep and all will be well."

Jack wanted to ask what she meant, but he supposed he would find out soon enough. He flinched as they walked into the spinning rings. Yet somehow the metal didn't touch them. He walked directly into the center of the rings and turned around. The silvery light was all around them now.

Everything outside the rings seemed to be moving in slow motion. Every blink of an eye took ten times longer than it should. He wanted to ask Elion what was happening, but the thrumming was so loud she wouldn't have heard him.

Jack looked down when he felt wetness around his ankles. Thick green liquid rose inside the spinning rings, and within seconds it was above his chest. Elion smiled at him, so he tried to pretend he wasn't afraid. But when the liquid continued to rise, he took a deep breath before it passed over his head.

Jack let go of Elion's hand and kicked frantically upward, but the liquid was far too thick for swimming. The world was darkness. Surely this couldn't be what was meant to happen! Jack's chest burned as the oxygen in his lungs was depleted. He gasped and inhaled deeply.

As he breathed in, his vision cleared. He was floating in an emerald sea—and it was exhilarating. Elion was beside him, wearing an amused look. When he tried to ask what was happening, only bubbles escaped his lips. Elion laughed as bubbles spilled from her mouth; her eyes changed from gold to aqua blue.

She pointed downward. Not far below, hundreds of streams were flowing through the emerald ocean. She motioned for Jack to follow and began swimming toward the closest stream. She swam directly into it and sped away in a beam of light.

Jack gasped, then kicked his legs and reached for the stream. The moment his fingers touched it, he was drawn inside and propelled forward. Suddenly he was moving so quickly he thought his skin might burn off from the sheer speed of it.

Just as Jack thought he could take it no longer, he saw a shimmering wall—and on the other side was land. Before he could see more, his skin pricked and he was tumbling across a jungle floor.

Elion laughed delightfully as Jack rolled to a stop. "There truly is nothing like traveling through the Sea of Worlds!"

Jack's stomach turned somersaults as he pulled himself up by a thick vine. "Where are we?" He gazed upward, feeling as small as an ant. Every tree was at least ten times bigger than any he'd seen before. They rose so high and had such large canopies it was impossible to see the sky. The ground was a tumble of roots and moss; massive vines hung everywhere.

"I would guess we are in the Brazilian rain forest," Elion said.

Jack had always loved maps and had dreamed of seeing new and faraway places. But Brazil was as far away from Ireland as he could imagine. His mind spun as he looked at the mammoth trees and low-hanging vines.

"Jack." Elion's voice was tight. "Don't move."

Jack had just seen what Elion saw, and though he wanted to scream, he did as told. He wasn't leaning against a giant vine but an unbelievably large snake. The serpent was twice as wide as Jack, with a head the size of a carriage wheel.

Elion stepped closer and spoke in a whisper. "Although this serpent is not a follower of the Assassin, it is still wild and therefore dangerous."

Jack didn't blink. The serpent's head hovered directly in front of his. Its eyes were locked on his while its great forked tongue flicked in and out, brushing against Jack's chin. The serpent's skin was golden with round black spots, and it shimmered as it moved.

When Elion stepped closer, the serpent hissed irritably, yet its gaze never left Jack. The Sephari hissed back. Except it wasn't just a hiss; it was more like a series of strange fizzling sounds. Her body swayed bonelessly.

She's talking to it! Jack's eyes widened. The snake seemed interested in whatever Elion was saying, though it continued to watch Jack. The conversation continued, and Jack's legs began to cramp. He felt like he'd been standing there for hours. Without warning, the giant serpent whipped back.

Jack dropped to his knees and screamed as the snake sprang forward and rushed past. The serpent's body was so long it took nearly ten seconds before it disappeared into the jungle.

"What ... what just happened?"

"I told the serpent who you are," Elion said. "I told it the Last Battle is coming and explained that nothing in this world will be able to stand aside. All living things must choose whom they will serve."

"You can speak to snakes?" Jack asked, still panting.

"Yes, I can speak to all creatures. Though some are far too stubborn to reason with."

"Why would a snake care who I am?"

"All of creation stands on the brink, Jack. The choice must be made, darkness or light, the Author or the Assassin." Elion looked in the direction the snake had disappeared. "I told the serpent it has a greater purpose. I asked if it would join the Awakened and help us spread the word of your and Alexia's arrival."

Jack gulped. "And what did it say?"

"It hasn't decided yet. Though it obviously decided not to eat you, so that was positive at least." Elion smiled. "But it can feel the battle coming. It can sense it in the air. By now every creature on earth knows the world is changing. The Last Battle is almost here. And though many still hope to escape it, in the end the choice must be made—darkness or light."

Chapter 11

UPSIDE DOWN

Days passed and Alexia was more mystified than ever. She wasn't a prisoner. In fact, she could do almost anything she wanted. The Assassin had even given her permission to go back to her friends. He'd just asked her to stay in Thaltorose a few weeks before making a decision.

Alexia had barely seen her father. He was too busy to see her, except for lunch a few times. And she was confused about him. Besides the way he looked and sounded, everything about him was different—even his name.

"Those who choose to serve the Shadow Lord are given a new name," her father had told her.

Is he really different, she wondered, *or have I just been remembering him wrong?* The thought came to Alexia each time they talked. She'd been only five years old, after all. Could she really remember him as well as she thought she did? Every day since the fire, she had dreamed about seeing her father. All she'd wanted was to sit on his lap and have him call her Alley Goat.

But her father hadn't called her Alley Goat once, and every time she was with him, he seemed preoccupied and irritable. Had she done something wrong or made him angry somehow?

Alexia was free to explore the palace and all of Thaltorose. Yet since the day the Assassin had opened the curtains, she'd been too afraid to even look out the window, let alone leave the palace. What she'd seen was burned into her memory.

The sky of Thaltorose was an unearthly yellow, and winged monsters filled the air. Black spires rose impossibly high, and the streets had been filled with shadows and sickly looking humans and creatures. But it hadn't been these things that scared Alexia so, at least not entirely. Everything about the city felt … hollow, as if a heavy wind could blow it all away. The buildings, the gold and gemstone streets, even the people and creatures had been lacking in … substance.

The palace, though unnerving at first, was becoming familiar. Like the room she slept in, the palace was solid gold and encrusted with every jewel imaginable. Every inch of it was glaringly bright. And though it should have been something from her dreams, it all still felt wrong somehow. She'd learned to ignore the shadows at the corners of her vision. Something dark always seemed to be slithering just out of sight, but whenever she turned to look, nothing was there.

Her father told her every servant in the palace belonged to her. "You can command them to do anything and they will do it," he'd said. "Tell any citizen of Thaltorose or any member of the Shadow Army to stop breathing—and they will."

Alexia's stomach had turned at her father's example, but it was true. At least so far. When Alexia was hungry, she could choose any servant in the palace and ask for food. At first it had been like a dream—ice cream and cake and sugar cookies and strawberry pie had come to her by the table load. Yet as the days passed, the whole thing began to feel absurd.

The only thing expected of her was to meet with the Assassin for a few hours every evening. It hadn't taken long to realize he was injured and sick. He tried to hide it, but his hand was often pressed against his stomach, and if he forgot to dab at his face with a kerchief, sweat dripped steadily from his chin. When he came near, the smell of rotting flesh emanated from his belly. Alexia guessed he'd gotten the wound when Jack had stabbed him in the stomach.

Alexia always met the Assassin in his throne room, which was enormous. Thousands of torches lined the walls, and at least fifty fire pits burned throughout. Gemstone-encrusted pillars rose to impossibly high ceilings; the floor was rich marble. Standing near the balcony was a golden statue of the Assassin, so enormous the head was lost in the shadows of the vaulted ceiling. Only its fiery eyes were visible from below. The golden throne was the size of a small house and encrusted with diamonds.

Each time Alexia walked in, she found the Assassin sitting atop the mammoth throne, caressing a small wooden box. It was not much larger than a fist and so plain that it looked completely out of place. Whenever Alexia entered the throne room, the Assassin would drop the box and turn his attention to her. The moment it left his fingers, the box floated beside him. As it hovered there, shadows detached from the throne and slithered around the box, making it almost impossible to see.

After the strange box was safely away, the Assassin would stand and walk down the golden stairs of the throne, extending his hand. Each time she wrapped her fingers around his, her skin crawled. Yet she made herself hold on because her father wanted her to get to know the Assassin. She spent hours walking through the throne room, talking with him.

During one visit, she found the courage to ask a question that had been burning in her since her arrival. "Did you kill Megan Staples?" she asked, feeling her chest tighten at the memory.

"I did not," the Assassin answered. "I came to Ballylesson to find you, my lady. And when I arrived, I saw the old woman you know as Mrs. Dumphry standing over the body. I can only assume she killed her." He shook his head sadly. "I am sorry, but I was too late to save her."

Alexia remembered walking out of the house and finding Megan lying on a sea of grass. A short while later, Mrs. Dumphry had arrived to take Alexia and Jack away. Could the Assassin be telling the truth?

"Why do they call you the Assassin?" she asked without thinking. As soon as the words left her mouth, she regretted them. For just a moment the Assassin's icy blue eyes became the caverns of fire she'd seen on her first day in Thaltorose.

"Those who call themselves the Awakened," he said, "gave me that name. They thought it a curse, but I have embraced it as an honor! My dear lady, there are few still living I have allowed to address me by my real name, but I would be pleased if you would call me Belial."

Alexia gulped, then quickly nodded. "Okay, Belial," she said. "Thank you. Did you really assassinate someone?"

"Yes, I did. But you must understand I had no choice. You see, there was a man, a very dangerous man, who called himself a simple poet." Belial grimaced. "And this poet, this treacherous man, threatened to topple the greatest kingdom this world has ever known."

He walked out to the balcony at the side of the throne room. Alexia hesitated. She didn't want to look at the city again. But Belial stayed silent, waiting for her to join him. After a moment she took a deep breath and marched out.

She gasped. The city was not nearly so terrifying as it had been that first night. Yes, the sky was an unearthly yellow, but there was something pleasant about it ... not quite beautiful, but impressive at least. And those weren't monsters filling the air, but strange, winged creatures, and there was something graceful about them.

The city was as gilded as the palace—streets paved in gold, studded with gemstones. Alexia stared in awe at the elegant black spires. The city still felt ... hollow, but it didn't bother her as she looked on it now.

"It's beautiful, isn't it?" Belial said.

"It is," Alexia lied. She could not call it beautiful, but it wasn't the nightmare she remembered. *I must have imagined it.*

"My lady, I know you have only been in Thaltorose a week, but you have already made me so happy. I am glad you agreed to stay, at least for a while. And though you have been here only a short time, have you seen how we live?"

Alexia nodded, suddenly dizzy as she looked into Belial's eyes. When he placed a hand on her shoulder, she shivered at his ice-cold touch. Yet when he spoke, his voice was somehow less jarring than she remembered.

"In my kingdom, anything you want is yours—riches beyond measure." He dabbed at the sweat dripping from his chin. "But this vicious man, this poet who pretended to stand for peace, threatened it all. He used honeyed words to turn the hearts of the people. And, my dear lady"—Belial grabbed Alexia's hands and knelt in front of her—"I had to have the man killed, don't you see? He threatened our entire way of life. He would have ruined everything!"

Belial turned his gaze on Thaltorose once again. "Those who followed this poet called me an Assassin, and they were right." For a moment Belial's eyes shifted to the fiery caverns. "And I would do it again. I do not regret it."

Alexia didn't know what to say. Belial admitted to killing someone. He didn't try to hide it, and he didn't treat her like a child. He offered answers to her questions. She wasn't sure what she thought, but this Belial didn't seem half so threatening as Mrs. Dumphry and Elion made him out to be. Even the smell of rotting flesh began to diminish as she looked into his eyes.

Chapter 12

A CHILD NO LONGER

Elion and Jack had been walking through the jungle for more than a week—a blessedly uneventful week, save for one evening.

Each night as they made camp, Jack trained with Ashandar for an hour or more. Elion made him train blindfolded, claiming he needed to "feel" the sword's movement. Yet only once had Jack felt the handle warm in his hands. Elion had told him not to move until he felt Ashandar prompting him to move. The sword knew battle more than he ever would, and if he listened, it would teach him. Then Elion left to collect wood for a fire.

Jack stood blindfolded, with Ashandar outstretched, for almost forty minutes, but all he felt was the biting bugs. He had been about to take the blindfold off when the sword began to warm. Ashandar called to him, and without thinking, Jack began to move.

There were no wild swings or leaps and kicks as he'd imagined; rather it was a steady flow of intricate strikes and twists of the blade. He gave himself to the sword. Somehow he moved among the thick roots without ever tripping. Jack felt as though he were dancing, both graceful and calculating.

Sweat poured from him and his muscles burned, yet the movements became more natural with each passing second. His breathing was labored, but he didn't slow. Ashandar was fire in his hands. As the movements became routine, he thought of his mother, father, and brother. He remembered everyone sitting around the kitchen table and laughing at one of Parker's jokes. He remembered building a giant snowman in his front yard with Parker and Father.

Jack continued to move, unsure whether he himself was moving his body or Ashandar was—until something changed. He froze, a feeling of terror rising inside him. Something evil had entered the jungle; he could feel the darkness pressing against him. A sickly sweet smell filled the air as bird and insect went eerily silent.

"NO MATTER WHERE YOU RUN, YOU WILL NOT ESCAPE ME."

Jack gasped. He knew this voice. Yet he couldn't make himself move. He wanted to remove the blindfold, to run, to scream for Elion, but his muscles wouldn't listen. Ashandar was fire in his hands, and the sword was willing him to stay perfectly still.

"YOUR DEATH WILL END THIS WAR, JACK STAPLES. BUT I WILL NOT STOP WITH YOU. I WILL DESTROY

EVERYONE YOU KNOW AND LOVE. YOUR FATHER AND BROTHER, YOUR FRIENDS …"

Jack barely breathed. Every word the Assassin spoke was like a knife in his heart. Ashandar called to him, and he lunged forward, extending the blade and twisting it upward. "No!" he screamed.

"NOOO!" the Assassin's scream echoed.

Jack stumbled as Ashandar cooled, and he landed flat on his face. He ripped the blindfold off and rolled onto his back. The jungle was perfectly normal now—insects chirping and birds calling. Before he could rise, Elion was there. She stood on the tips of her toes, with a short sword in her hands. Her hair glowed with a golden light, and her eyes were silvery gold.

"What happened?" Her voice was tight.

Jack told her everything. When he finished, Elion sheathed her sword. "I will not pretend to understand what just happened, and I do not doubt what you heard, but it may not have been the Assassin. Yet I'm sure we'll find out soon enough." She scanned the surrounding jungle and offered Jack a hand. "For now at least, I think the danger has passed."

Most of his evenings were pleasantly uneventful. After he trained with Ashandar, Jack sat around a fire with Elion and talked. And each night Jack asked as many questions as he could before he fell asleep from exhaustion. One night he asked Elion how long it would take to get to the garden.

"I don't know," she said. "The Forbidden Garden is never where you found it last."

"Then how do you find it?"

"So long as you believe you are walking toward it, you will arrive eventually. But you must believe."

"But how does it move? I don't understand."

"The garden doesn't move exactly, but it is always where it needs to be. And apparently it needs to be in Brazil right now."

Jack was excited to finally be getting answers. Most answers Elion gave only brought new questions, but she seemed happy to answer anything he asked.

The next night, Jack and Elion sat around a small fire, roasting a rabbit on a stick. "Elion, can you tell me what's truly happening? I don't understand most of it." He was so confused most of the time that he didn't know what to ask.

Elion stared into the fire. "Do you know what an Oriax is, Jack?"

"I don't think so." He was puzzled by the question. "I guess I thought they were from your world, something the Assassin created—something evil."

"The Assassin does not have the power to create, only to distort." Elion's eyes became a thunderstorm. "Every Oriax was once a normal animal."

"But how can an animal change like that?"

"As I keep telling you, all creation must make the choice: Will I follow the Author or will I become enslaved to the Assassin?"

"But what does that have to do with Oriax?"

"When humans choose evil, your souls become distorted. But for animals the distortions are on the outside.

"The Assassin wants to remake the world in his image. And his is a world without mercy. When men or animals choose to follow him, at first they like what they find. They are offered power and riches;

they are shown a world without rules. But power will never satisfy. It is a sickness. The more you have, the more you want. And riches have no more meaning than a tool, like a hammer or saw."

Jack remembered Agartha. Diamonds and silver had been placed inside the stone to help strengthen the city. To the Awakened, a diamond was no more valuable than a stone.

"It doesn't take long for those who follow the Assassin to realize they have become his slaves. They seek power but will never hold enough. They gain riches but are never satisfied. They chase glory and become consumed by jealousy. So when the Assassin demands that his followers murder, steal, and destroy in order to find more power, wealth, and glory, they do it. And their souls become even more distorted."

Jack was cold as he listened to her words.

"An Oriax is merely a beast that has given itself fully to the Assassin. It has killed again and again. And what it kills it devours. And what it devours it becomes."

Jack shivered.

Elion reached into a small bag and produced some bread and cheese. "Once an animal begins to change, it will seek out its new master. The Oriax can find their masters—Shadule, Drogule, and Grendalls—in the same way a homing pigeon finds its way home."

As Elion spoke, the fire sent shadows dancing across her face. "The world changed when you stabbed the Assassin. He cannot heal from a wound given by Ashandar. Even now the evil spills from him, and where it blows, insanity follows."

"I didn't know." Jack was horrified. "I didn't mean to ... I would never have ...."

"You need not apologize. It was inevitable that the Assassin's evil would spread. But he is also wounded, and that is a good thing! No matter how many followers he finds, the Assassin is our true enemy. I tell you this because you need to know that just because the scales have fallen from someone's eyes, it does not make him or her good. We must choose the right thing even when our eyes are open."

"Like the man," Jack said. "Like Korah."

A troubled look entered Elion's eyes. "Yes, like Korah. He was once one of us. He was a member of the Council of Seven and more zealous than most. But he refused instruction and did not seek wisdom. I fear what he will do to Alexia."

Jack's chest tightened. Every time he thought of Alexia, he struggled to breathe. She was his friend. And knowing Alexia was out there, knowing she was also special, made Jack feel less alone. "Will the Assassin hurt her? Will he torture her?"

"Yes, he will hurt her," Elion said, "but not in the way you are thinking. The Assassin is a master of distortion and manipulation. What Alexia once saw as evil will become entertainment, and what once sickened may eventually satisfy."

With each passing day, Alexia was feeling more comfortable in Thaltorose. She no longer dreaded her time with Belial. But she was surprised to find that her least favorite hours were those spent with her father. He was so different.

Alexia rose from her massive bed and reached for her cloak and sling, then stopped. Her heart sank—her cloak and sling were gone. The Atherial Cloak had been missing since she'd first awoken in Thaltorose—and now this. In place of her familiar clothing was a black-and-silver uniform just like her father's.

Tears welled in her eyes. The evening before, Alexia had gone to the war chamber to meet her father. Here, too, the floor was marble and the walls studded with gemstones, but the chamber also housed thousands of weapons.

There were barbed spears, spiked axes, and razor-encrusted halberds. There were balls of steel that exploded when thrown and swords with spiked pommels. There were whips with nine tails, each ending in something sharp. The walls were filled with more weapons than Alexia could have imagined.

As she stood gaping, her father entered behind her. "A sling is a child's toy," he'd snarled. "It was fine for a small girl, but you are older now and must learn how to fight with a real weapon."

"But you made me this sling!" Alexia said. "And I'm quite good with it. I practice every day."

Her father snatched the sling away and tossed it aside. "Do you want to be a little girl forever?"

She was heartbroken, but she didn't want to disappoint him. She walked to the wall and retrieved a thin sword with a rounded blade. He nodded approvingly at the weapon and then drew his own bone-white sword. They trained for hours—and her father was an exceptionally harsh teacher. He never showed her something more than once, and when she did something wrong, he screamed at her.

At the end of the training, her father had called to her. "One more thing, Daughter." She turned to face him, hoping to hear just one word of encouragement. "You need a new cloak," he said. "If you are to rule this city, you must dress appropriately."

"No!" Alexia gasped. "This was made from the dress Mother made me. I don't want to stop wearing it!"

"Do not cross me, girl," he said. "I expect obedience and perfection from you. Or are these things too much to ask?"

Alexia backed away. "Please, Father, let me keep it!"

Her father looked at her a moment, then shook his head. "You are a young woman now. Every time you act like a child, you shame me." Without another word he ripped the cloak and sling from her arms and stalked away. That night, Alexia had cried herself to sleep.

Now Alexia sat in her bed feeling sick as she stared at the uniform. *I need to grow up*, she thought bitterly. *I'm not a little girl anymore, and I can't just sit in bed and cry!*

Until now Alexia had spent her days exploring the palace. But she was growing bored with staying inside, and though she was starting to enjoy her times with Belial, she only met him at the end of the day. Besides answering her questions, Belial had begun teaching her how to control her gifts. In addition to having agility and balance, he claimed, Alexia could manipulate animals. He said she could control them if she learned how. This excited her more than anything. But there were no animals in the palace to try to control.

Alexia dressed hurriedly and tried not to think of her cloak and sling as she left her room. She didn't bother summoning a servant. She was still full from the meal of spiced lamb, potatoes, chicken potpie, apple pie, and ice cream she'd had the night before. Today

Alexia planned to finally explore Thaltorose. She wanted to find some animals to see if she could control them. *If the city really is mine*, she thought, *I should at least see it.* When she stepped out of the palace courtyard and onto the city street, Alexia gaped.

Thaltorose was absolutely spectacular. The yellow sky seemed somehow more natural than before, and it was filled with magical flying creatures. The streets and buildings were covered in ornate gold and silver scrollwork. And though it still felt hollow, she'd learned to ignore that bit.

As she walked the streets, Alexia wondered if Thaltorose was like Belfast. *Are there two cities here? Are there street urchins and gangs who rule the night? Or is it like Agartha?* Although she'd spent much of her time in Agartha trying to escape, she had never once seen a starving face or someone skulking in the shadows.

Mountains surrounded Thaltorose, but they had a different sort of beauty. Belial's servants had mined them in search of the gold and gems that ornamented the city. The mountains had been transformed into dark craters or were filled with holes and pockmarks. But there was still something grand about them.

As she walked farther from the palace, Alexia couldn't see any signs of a second city. Every building was glaringly extravagant. There wasn't a butcher or barbershop that wasn't encrusted with precious metal or jewels. Impressive spires rose spectacularly high, and exotic creatures walked and slithered alongside men and women.

There were no hungry faces or pickpockets, but something about the people felt odd. No matter how far she walked, Alexia couldn't shake the feeling of being watched. Yet every time she turned around … there was nobody there. Equally eerie, everyone seemed to know who she was. They smiled and bowed as she walked past, but there was no mistaking the fear behind their eyes. The more Alexia saw, the more she couldn't shake the feeling of wrongness.

There are no children! The thought made Alexia stop. She'd been walking for hours and hadn't seen a single child. *And no one is laughing.* Everyone smiled, but there was no joy in it. The more she walked, the uneasier she became.

What's wrong with everyone? And what kind of city has no children? The men, women, and strange creatures felt unnatural, with their bright colors, gaudy jewelry, pale faces, and dead eyes. As she passed a particularly large building, Alexia glanced inside to see a large structure of interlocking silvery rings. *It's just like the one beneath Buckingham Palace,* she thought. She was certain it was a World Portal. Mrs. Dumphry had planned on taking her and Jack and the others through one of these so they could flee the Assassin. The thought made Alexia furious; Belial had been far more gracious with her than Mrs. Dumphry had ever been. He treated her like a proper lady.

Belial told her Mrs. Dumphry had killed Megan Staples, and the more Alexia thought about it, the more she thought it might be true. *She's the reason Jack and Arthur and I got caught up in all of this! All she ever did was treat us like children. I bet she was lying about all of it!*

Alexia glanced around to be sure no one was watching. She wanted to go somewhere to think, somewhere no one could see her. *Now!* She darted down a side passage and quickly climbed onto the roof of a nearby shop.

I think it's time for a little eavesdropping, she thought with a grin. As she ran along the rooftops, she smiled for the first time in days.

This was where she felt most at home. Yet after an hour of listening from the eaves, Alexia hadn't heard a single conversation. The people of Thaltorose were utterly silent. They walked the streets with those unnatural smiles that never reached their eyes, but they didn't say a word to one another. *Come to think of it, none of them spoke to me unless I spoke to them first*, Alexia realized. *And even then they only answered my questions.*

The hairs on Alexia's neck stirred as she walked up a particularly steep roof. When she reached the top, she saw it. Hidden away in a corner of the city, standing bold against the horizon, was the arena that had haunted her dreams almost every night since her fifth birthday. The mammoth coliseum made of sleek black stone called to Alexia, willing her to come.

Jack forced his eyes to stay open. He and Elion had been walking for ten days, and Elion had no idea how much farther they would need to go before they reached the Forbidden Garden.

"Elion, will you tell me about my family?" he asked, trying to hide a yawn. "Do you know where my father and Parker are now? Do they know what's happened? Do they know about Mother and the town?"

"I honestly don't know, Jack. All I've been able to learn is your father and brother weren't in Ballylesson when the Oriax attacked because they had been sent on a very important mission. And before you ask"—Elion smiled—"I don't know what their mission was or who gave it to them or where they are now. But I can promise you this—they are as desperate to see you as you are to see them."

Jack turned and stirred the coals of the fire with a long stick. He had been told his father and Parker were gone because they were working on a masonry project. "Why wasn't I told?" he asked. "Why was I the only one who didn't know? If I'm so important, why didn't Mother or Father trust me enough to tell me about all of this when I was younger?" The stick snapped in his hand.

"I know you're angry. And perhaps we were wrong not to tell you sooner. But you must understand that knowledge is dangerous. And knowing that you carry the fate of the world on your shoulders is enough to make the bravest warrior tremble in fear." As Elion grabbed Jack's hand, her eyes shifted through a rainbow of colors.

"We do not know what comes next or what will be asked of you. And while there is an answer to every question under the sun, it is not answers that brings peace, but trust. We must trust the Author."

"Trust the Author?" Jack threw his broken stick into the jungle. "Everyone's always talking about this stupid Author. And I've never even met him! I don't even know who he is. How can you expect me to trust him?"

"This is the most important question you have asked so far. But I am afraid I will not answer it."

"What?" Jack said.

"I am taking you to the Forbidden Garden so you can meet with Time. She wants to show you something. And what she shows you will answer these questions better than I ever could."

Chapter 13

THE GANG OF ROGUES

Alexia thought longingly of her Atherial Cloak as she sprinted across a rooftop toward the arena of black stone. And then—*Wild!* Alexia almost stumbled at the thought. How could she have forgotten about him? Wild had risked his life to save her. *I'll have to ask Father when I get back to the palace.* She shook off the feeling of guilt and continued forward.

As she neared the edge of the roof, Alexia dropped to her belly and crawled the rest of the way. Black rock stretched high, forming archways that became lost in the clouds. The entire coliseum looked to be carved out of a single mountain.

Alexia wanted to sneak inside the arena and see the place that had haunted her dreams for as long as she could remember. Yet she was also afraid of what she would find. *I never thought it was real!*

She had just decided to climb down when a filthy boy in tattered clothes sprinted out of an entryway. He skidded to a stop and scanned the surroundings.

Before he could decide on a direction, four Oriax charged from the same corridor and quickly surrounded him. The beasts snarled and hissed as he turned, trying to watch all four at the same time.

"Come and get me!" he screamed. "I'm not afraid of you!" But the Oriax didn't attack; they waited, circling to ensure he didn't run. A moment later a Shadule slithered out.

"I warned you what would happen if you tried to escape again." The creature moved with liquid grace. "Take him to the crack," it said. The beasts growled and lunged at the boy to corral him back toward the arena.

"No, please! I promise I won't do it again," he cried. "I was just hungry; we all are. We need something to eat!" The Oriax snarled and swiped their claws, forcing him into the corridor until he disappeared from view.

Alexia let out a long, shuddering breath. She knew this boy. It was Josiah, and he was her friend.

Six years earlier

Alexia stared at the beige sheet of paper. She could barely believe it. Josiah hunched next to her, rocking on his heels excitedly. "Five pounds!" he almost shouted. "That's enough to buy a horse, for goodness sake!"

Josiah had ripped the paper from a lantern post earlier that evening. The page showed an extremely good drawing of Alexia Dreager, and at the bottom were the words "This child is extremely dangerous: A five pound reward for information leading to her arrest."

"Five pounds!" Alexia said. It truly was a ridiculous amount of money. "But why?"

Sitting nearby were four more children who were all close in age: Juno, Summer, and Benaiah were six, and Adeline had just turned five. Alexia had been living with Josiah and the others for the past few days. The children called themselves the Gang of Misfits, which Alexia thought was an absurd name.

In truth, they were five street kids who had no place to go and no one to look after them. Either their parents had died or they were runaways. The children had found one another somehow and looked after each other as best they could.

Josiah had brought Alexia here after they'd escaped from Korah and his Gang of Terror. She'd stayed because she was too heartbroken to go anywhere else. Their hideout was in an abandoned factory in the most dangerous slum in Belfast.

Alexia hated Korah more than she'd ever hated anyone. The man had ruined her beloved dress! She now wore brown pants and a cream-colored shirt. They were tattered and worn, and she hated them too.

Alexia looked at the five dirty faces around her. *I don't need these kids getting in my way*, she told herself for the twentieth time. *I should just leave. It's not safe here anyway, not with Korah looking for me.* But every time she thought of leaving, the look in Josiah's eyes made her stay just one more day.

"Why does Lord Korah want you so badly?" Juno asked. "There's no reward for Josiah."

Juno was a small girl with white hair and a thick accent. She was quick on her feet and even quicker with her hands. That very morning Alexia had seen her pick the pockets of five men in less than two minutes.

"I don't know what he wants," Alexia said. Ever since she and Josiah escaped the Gang of Terror, she'd heard rumors that they were looking for her. But five pounds!

"Does this mean you're going to leave us, then?" Josiah asked.

Alexia didn't know how to answer. She liked these children. Josiah and his friends looked up to her; it made her feel important and responsible for them. "I don't know," she said. "I think we should get some sleep now. We can talk about it in the morning."

While the children unrolled their blankets and curled up on the floor, Alexia tried to ignore the guilt that was growing inside her. But as she readied herself for bed, she made her decision. She would sleep a few hours, then wake early and sneak away. These kids would have to make do without her.

Sleep came almost instantly. Like most nights, she had the same dream of the red wildflowers, the massive arena, the three gravestones. She opened her eyes to see the sun peeking through the broken window— she'd overslept. It would be far harder to leave when the children were awake. She sat up and immediately spotted her opened satchel.

It's gone! Alexia stood in a rage. "Where is it? Where is my dress?" she screamed.

The children sat up groggily.

"I have it!" Juno called from another room.

Alexia stalked toward Juno, who held the red dress out to her. Alexia shoved Juno with all her might, screaming, "How dare you steal my dress!"

"I didn't steal it, Blade, really! I tried to fix it!" Juno cowered on the floor.

Alexia stopped. She held the dress up and was confused by what she saw.

"I couldn't figure out how to fix the dress, so I used the pieces to make a cloak ... I'm sorry, I thought you would like it; I wanted to surprise you!"

Alexia fingered the crimson cloak. She'd been on the verge of tears for days now. But Juno hadn't stolen her dress—she had fixed it, rather. She'd transformed it! Alexia studied the stitching; it was beautiful.

"My grandmother was a seamstress," Juno said. "She taught me how to sew before she died. I thought you would like it or I never would have taken it, really!"

"I love it," Alexia whispered, suddenly teary. "It's perfect."

She tried it on. The cloak fit perfectly!

"I'm sorry I pushed you. I shouldn't have done that," Alexia said. "I'll never forget what you did for me."

Juno smiled as Alexia pulled her to her feet. "It's the strangest thing," Juno said. "It never should have been enough to make the cloak, but ... there was exactly enough. It is a very peculiar material. I know it sounds crazy, but it's like it wanted me to make it into a cloak. Do you know what it is?"

Alexia had no idea, though she'd often wondered. The dress seemed to have a life of its own. She'd worn it for more than two years and it had still fit perfectly. Until Korah had destroyed it, the dress was still as good as new.

Alexia stood proudly and looked at the rest of the children. "If I'm going to stay with you and lead this gang, then we need a better name," she said. "From now on we will be known as the Gang of Rogues, and we will rule this city!"

All five children jumped and cheered wildly, dancing about as they whooped and hollered in excitement.

Present day

Alexia was horrified as she watched the Oriax escort Josiah back into the coliseum. *Why would anyone kidnap an orphan boy from Belfast?* Her mind spun as she turned and raced toward the palace. She was meant to meet with Belial before the sun set, and unless she hurried, she was sure to be late.

Although she hated leaving him, Alexia knew she couldn't just run in and rescue Josiah. She needed time to think, to make a plan. Maybe it was a misunderstanding. Maybe she could tell her father or Belial and they would release her friend.

Maybe they don't even know he's being held prisoner! she thought. *Belial told me I could ask for anything and he would do it. I'll ask for Josiah's freedom!*

At the palace, she began to climb. She wasn't thinking as she leaped between two balconies and continued upward. The balcony to the throne room was fifty stories up, and she was in a hurry. It was far quicker to climb the outside of the palace than to run through the maze of endless corridors. Up, up, higher she went. Her fingertips curled around a slim edge of stone. Her heel hooked around the body of a gargoyle. Then, as she pulled herself up to perch on the windowsill, Alexia suddenly realized what she was doing.

What am I thinking? She was forty-eight stories up! When Alexia looked down at what she'd just climbed, she gasped. Suddenly dizzy, she leaned against the palace wall. She had great balance, but this was ridiculous.

Alexia pulled aside a heavy curtain and peered into a large chamber. Torches lined walls gilded in tanzanite, and elaborate tapestries hung from arched ceilings. Alexia stepped quietly inside, planning to walk through to the corridor.

"Father," she whispered, as dread rose in her belly.

Every tapestry in the chamber depicted different scenes of her father just moments away from killing someone. In each tapestry he wielded a bone-white sword and had a look of ecstasy in his eyes. His victims' faces showed only terror.

I must be in Father's chamber! She had never been allowed to come to him and hadn't been able to find where he stayed. Fear coursed through her as she walked past hundreds of tapestries into an adjoining chamber that held her father's bed. Next to the bed was a large number of skulls, a mixture of animal and human. Alexia shuddered. She hadn't realized she was afraid of her father until this moment. But now she was terrified.

She fingered a skull that could have belonged to an Oriax. Lying next to it was a black chain with a small, blue-veined stone at the end. As she looked closer at the stone, she saw something moving inside.

"How could you lose her?"

Alexia jumped at the sound of her father's voice. She pocketed the stone without thinking and darted out of the bedchamber toward the outer window. Her father had entered from another room.

"Your only job is to watch a little girl—and you lost her in a city that we control?"

"I was watching her closely, master." Whatever was speaking had a distinctly whiney voice. "But then she went to the rooftops. The girl is fast. I couldn't keep up!"

Alexia stood frozen in the center of the outer chamber. She had been running to the windowsill when she'd spotted the largest tapestry in the room. It was huge and showed her father holding a blade to her mother's neck. Lying at their feet was another man. Alexia could only see the back of his head.

What? Horror and confusion churned inside her.

"No!" the creature whimpered as something crashed to the floor.

Alexia darted to the window, quickly stepping onto the sill and out of sight.

"I do not accept failure," her father said cruelly as he entered the chamber of tapestries.

"P-p-please?" the creature whimpered. Alexia peeked around the corner of the window. Her father was standing with his back to her, his sword in his hands. The whimpering creature had seen her. Its one eye opened wide in surprise. It began to point in her direction—

Alexia squeezed her eyes shut. She heard the chunk of the sword and the sound of something falling to the ground and rolling away. She trembled but didn't wait. She leaped from the sill and grabbed the head of a beastly gargoyle. Panic and confusion roared inside her as she began to climb once again.

Alexia needed to be away from her father. She needed to think about the tapestry, and she needed to get to Belial. The sun had already set, and she was late.

Chapter 14

THE GUARDIANS' RIDDLE

Jack stood at the edge of the jungle, hidden behind a gigantic tree. "What do you mean, you're leaving?"

"I cannot enter the Forbidden Garden, Jack. That is your quest. There are other things I must attend to now." Elion turned and looked toward the south. "I will go to the City of Shadows. I fear our friends may need my help if they are to survive."

"So you're just going to leave me here? I'm the Child of Prophecy. You're supposed to take care of me, to keep me safe!"

"Have I not done so?" Elion's voice was more warm than chiding. "No Sephari can enter the Forbidden Garden. To do so would be death."

Just beyond the trees a small expanse of sand spilled into the ocean. A short distance beyond was an island barely large enough to house a tiny log cabin. A thin plume of smoke rose from the cabin.

"And I am afraid it is worse than you think. You should know that almost all who have tried to enter the Forbidden Garden have died gruesome deaths," Elion said. "The Author has placed two guardians to keep watch over the garden. Only those who are deemed worthy shall pass. The guardians will present you with a test; it may be a riddle or a task of some sort. Should you pass, you will be allowed to swim to the cabin. Should you fail, they will kill you."

Jack's jaw dropped in disbelief. The world started spinning as he waited for Elion to say more, but nothing came. "I don't understand," he said finally. "You brought me here so the guardians could kill me? What kind of test? And why do I have to meet with Time?"

"I do not believe you will die. The Author has great plans for you so I have to believe you will pass the test. And you must meet with Time because there are things you must see that only she can show you. I do not know what comes next. But I believe you are ready for this test. I believe in you, Jack Staples." Elion looked toward the south again. "But I must leave now. Do you have any last questions for me?"

Jack could think of a thousand questions, but he shook his head. Elion's eyes blazed with a silvery light. "You will do well." She cupped his chin. "You were born for this. To be right here, right now, is your destiny. But you must not delay; step out from behind this tree as soon as I leave." Elion stepped away and bowed her head. "Until we meet again." Without another word she turned and walked into the jungle.

Jack stood in stunned silence, watching the spot where he'd lost sight of Elion. When he turned to look back at the tiny cabin, he was surprised to see it was getting late. The sun hung low on the horizon, painting the world the color of blood.

He wanted to run back and scream for Elion. But he knew she was gone. So he studied the ocean. Everything looked completely normal. *Maybe she's wrong. Maybe I can swim to the cabin and just walk in.*

Deciding it would be far worse to make the swim in the dark, Jack took a deep breath, closed his eyes, and stepped out of the jungle. Nothing happened. He took a cautious step forward, then another as he walked to the water's edge and stepped in. Hope rose in his chest as he continued forward. *Maybe the guardians aren't here, after all!*

But the ocean began to bubble and churn as something enormous rose from its depths. The ground rolled and knocked Jack to his knees. He screamed and tried to stand. The sand was also churning as something colossal ascended from the ground. Water and sand showered down. Jack gasped for breath as murky saltwater spilled down his throat, threatening to drown him. Then the boiling stopped as suddenly as it had started.

Jack wiped sand from his eyes. He was paralyzed by fear. He stood sandwiched between two gigantic … somethings. The guardians were identical except for the colors of their scaled skin. They stood taller than the jungle trees and had the look of both lizard and eagle.

"Who dares disturb our rest?" the water guardian bellowed. Its scales were silvery green and its voice so thunderous Jack almost covered his ears. The guardian shook its birdlike head, and more water cascaded down.

From his knees, Jack yelled, "My name is …" He coughed, spitting mud. "My name is Jack Staples and I am here to meet with Time!"

"Jack Staples?" the guardian behind him boomed. Its scales were red and gold, and as it spoke, its long, sinuous neck glided down so it could get a better look.

Jack was petrified. The guardian's eye was as big as he was. "What kind of creature is a Jack Staples?" the guardian rumbled. One of its two sets of eyelids flicked closed and then opened again, its gigantic pupil focused on Jack.

"I'm not a creature. I am a human!" Jack tried his best to sound brave.

"A human, you say?" the guardian boomed. "You are small for a human."

The other guardian, with silvery scales, lowered its head, eyeing Jack closer. "He is a puny thing!" it bellowed. "Aren't most humans bigger than you?"

"I'm just a boy," Jack said defensively, standing as tall as he could.

The golden guardian made a noise as loud as thunder. Jack covered his ears as the silvery guardian joined in. It was so loud that the earth began to tremble.

They're laughing at me! "I may be a child," he screamed, "but I am the Child of Prophecy and I demand you let me in to meet with Time!"

The guardians stopped laughing and lowered their heads to examine Jack once again. "The Child of Prophecy, you say?" the silvery guardian boomed. "We shall see. Maybe you are and maybe you are not. Thousands have tried to enter the Forbidden Garden, but few have ever done so. Do you think you will pass our test, Jack Staples?"

Jack swallowed hard. "What happened to the rest of them?"

The silvery guardian growled. "We get hungry, waiting here so long."

"In the olden days a warrior came every month. But we have not eaten in over a hundred years. We are famished, Jack Staples."

"And though you are small," the silvery guardian said, "we will savor your taste."

Jack turned warily as both guardians leaned forward in anticipation.

"We have a riddle for you," the golden guardian thundered.

"Answer correctly and you may enter the Forbidden Garden. Answer incorrectly and we will dine on you before the sun sets," the silvery guardian roared.

"No!" Jack screamed. "That's not enough time! The sun will be down in just a few minutes!"

"These have always been the rules. Surely you were told not to delay?" the golden guardian bellowed.

"Yes, I was told to come right away, but I wasn't ready. I wanted to think about it first!"

"The rules do not change because you are not ready. You must answer by sundown or die," the silvery guardian said.

Jack wanted to scream as he turned to look at the sinking sun. The bottom of the golden sphere was already touching the horizon.

"Answer this riddle," the golden guardian said, "and you may pass without delay."

The silvery guardian continued. "What is used every day but totally invisible? With it you can see the impossible, but without it, you would be utterly alone. It grows bigger with time but can be destroyed in a moment."

Jack's heart sank. Arthur was brilliant with riddles. Back in Ballylesson Arthur used to ask Jack a new riddle every day. He had a whole book of them. But Jack had never once gotten the answer right.

The silvery guardian looked at the sun. "You have four minutes before the sun sets, Jack Staples."

"No! You have to give me more time. That's not nearly enough. I don't even know where to begin!" But the guardians merely looked at him with hungry eyes.

Jack sank to his knees. "If it's not visible, then it can't be something physical." His mind raced. "With it I can see the impossible, and without it I would be alone." Jack had no idea what this meant.

"Three minutes left." The golden guardian smacked its gums hungrily.

Jack trembled. "If it helps me see the impossible, then it must be a good thing. But if I don't have it, I am alone. So whatever it is, it helps me get friends or something ..." Jack searched the guardians' eyes for any sign that he was right, but they merely stared at him, unblinking.

I'm utterly alone right now! His thoughts were becoming frenzied. *Where are my friends now? How could Elion just leave me here?*

Jack quickly skipped to the next part of the riddle. "It grows bigger with time," he said aloud. "This must mean it's like a muscle.

The more I use it, the bigger and stronger it becomes." He was pacing now, his mind turning somersaults.

"Two minutes before the sun sets," the silvery guardian rumbled.

Jack pushed them out of his mind. *Did Elion plan this all along? Did she want me to die?*

No. Jack took a breath, trying not to think about the fading light. "It can be destroyed in a moment ..." He repeated the last part of the riddle, but he couldn't think straight. He thought despairingly of his mother. "If Mother were here, she would help me, but she left!" he screamed. "Now I am alone!"

Hot tears ran down his cheeks, and as the last rays of the sun sank low on the horizon, the guardians rose higher, staring down at Jack as if he were an ant about to be stepped on.

"One minute until darkness comes," the golden guardian rumbled. "One minute until the feasting begins!"

"Mother left me and now all I have is Elion!" Jack cried. "I thought she cared. I thought—"

In that moment, Jack remembered something. On the morning his mother died, just before he discovered her body, he'd fainted and gone back in time. He found his mother in the kitchen, and she immediately rushed him outside so he wouldn't be seen. It had been snowing and the wind blew wildly.

Jack had tried to warn her that she was going to die, but she wouldn't listen. She'd knelt beside him and told him she loved him. She hugged him fiercely and kissed him on the cheek. And then she had told him to find Elion. "You can trust her above all," she'd whispered.

In the fading light the guardians became beasts of pure terror. Row upon row of fangs lined their eagle-like beaks, each fang two times bigger than Jack. And as the last rays of light faded, the guardians growled in anticipation.

"Trust!" Jack screamed at the top of his lungs. "The answer is trust!" Turning quickly so he could keep both guardians in view, Jack screamed for the third time. "Trust is used every day, in every relationship. But it is not visible!" Jack talked as fast as an avalanche. The last rays of the sun had disappeared and he desperately hoped he wasn't too late.

"If we trust with all our hearts, it gives us the confidence to try the impossible! And if we don't allow ourselves to trust, we will be alone. The more we trust someone, the more the trust grows. But no matter how big it gets, if someone betrays you, trust is destroyed!" Jack struggled to breathe as he waited to hear if he'd gotten the answer right.

Both guardians began sinking downward, as sand and water churned once again. Jack fell to his knees, unable to keep his body from shaking.

As the silvery guardian sank lower, it looked at Jack. "I am glad we did not have to eat you," it boomed. "We have awaited your arrival since time before time. Be strong, Jack Staples. Be strong and have courage. The end is near; the choice will be made; the Last Battle comes," it thundered as it disappeared beneath the waves.

Chapter 15

THE GREAT PILFERAGE

"Where have you been, my lady?" Belial offered a waxy smile. "I have been worried about you."

"I was walking in the city and I lost track of time," Alexia said. "I am sorry, Belial. It won't happen again."

Alexia was still breathless from her climb. She'd climbed into a higher window and raced to the throne room. Her mind spun as she thought about the tapestry in her father's chamber. *Why would Father hold a sword to Mother's neck? And who was the man on the ground?*

Belial waved a hand. "I am not angry, my Alexia. I merely wanted to be sure you were all right. I look forward to our times together."

Alexia sat down on a padded chair opposite Belial. They were sitting on the balcony of the throne room, gazing at the city. She schooled her face and tried to steady her breathing.

"What is it?" Belial patted the sweat on his brow. "I can see you have something on your mind. What troubles you?"

Alexia thought a moment and was surprised to find she was actually starting to like Belial. He had only been kind to her since she'd arrived in the city. Even the sickly smell emanating from him didn't seem quite so bad today.

"I did explore the city, and it is wonderful; truly it is." Alexia took a deep breath. "But when I was out, I saw something I didn't understand."

"What is it, my lady? What did you see?"

"It looked like an arena, and—" Alexia halted at the cold look in Belial's eyes.

"The coliseum is off limits." He dabbed at the bead of sweat dangling from his chin. "You were not meant to see it yet."

"I didn't know it was off limits or I never would have gone," Alexia lied. "But I did go, and when I was there, I saw something …" She hesitated.

"It is all right; I am not angry with you. I just didn't want you to see the coliseum for a few more days yet. I had planned to take you there myself. It was meant to be a surprise." Belial smiled. "Tell me what you saw and I will see if I can explain it to you."

A surprise for me? Alexia kept waiting for Belial to act like the Assassin she'd heard so much about. She expected horns to grow out of his head and fire to explode from his eyes, but he was always kind, and she rarely saw fire in his eyes anymore.

Alexia swallowed hard before continuing. "I saw a boy dressed in rags running from a Shadule and four Oriax. His name is Josiah and he was my friend when I lived in Belfast." For a moment Belial's eyes did become caverns of fire, but they shifted back to an icy blue so quickly Alexia wondered if she'd imagined it.

"The Shadule took him prisoner and took him back into the coliseum," Alexia said hastily. "I don't know what they want with him, but I know he's not bad. He does steal sometimes, but that's only because he doesn't have anything and his parents are gone. But he is good, I promise you!"

Belial stood, grimacing as he turned away from Alexia, and spoke in a careful tone. "And what would you have me do with this boy?"

"The thing is, you said I could ask anything I wanted and you would give it to me," Alexia said. "I want you to release him! I ask that you set Josiah free and let him come stay with me." Her voice quavered.

Belial turned, and Alexia was shocked to see tears in his eyes. He dropped to his knees and took her hands. It was the first time she didn't feel the need to shiver when he touched her. It was the first time she didn't notice his frigid, sweaty fingers or the putrid smell.

"My darling Alexia, my sweet, sweet lady, you could ask me anything, up to half my kingdom, and it would be yours—riches beyond your imagination, fame and power that would make kings quake in fear. Ask any of these things and I will gladly give them to you! But I cannot do this."

Alexia opened her mouth, ready to protest, but before she could speak, Belial continued. "My darling, it is not that I don't want to do this thing. It is that I cannot. Your friend Josiah now calls himself one of the Awakened. If he truly wants to be free, all he needs do is embrace me as king and you as the High Princess of Thaltorose. If he would bend his knee and bow before us, I would release him immediately. But the boy refuses!"

Belial stood, and this time he didn't try to hide the cavernous fire in his eyes. "Do you remember when I told you why they named me Assassin?"

Alexia nodded fearfully.

"I killed a poet because he tried to overthrow my kingdom. These creatures who call themselves Awakened have the same goal. All I have built here, all I am, they wish to destroy. My dear lady, how can I be expected to free someone who would destroy me if he had the chance? How could you ask me to do such a thing?"

Alexia shook her head, wiping tears from her eyes. Nothing made sense anymore. "I know he wouldn't try to hurt you if you let him go," she said. "I'm sure of it!"

"Your father follows me," Belial said. "Is that not enough? It was the Awakened who killed your mother; it was the Awakened who stole your father from you for all those years. I am the one who returned him to you. My dear lady, I will give you more power than you could possibly imagine. Together, we will rule this world! How could you ask me to free those who would stand in the way of what you want?"

"It's not that, Belial. I promise, I didn't mean that," Alexia said. "But let me talk to Josiah! I know I could change his mind if you give me the chance."

Belial sighed gratefully. "Of course you may see him! My darling, you are the High Princess of Thaltorose. You can do anything your heart desires! And if you can convince this boy to kneel before us and reject our enemies, I will embrace him with open arms. But if you cannot change his mind, then you must allow me to do with him as I wish. You must trust me wholly in this. Will you give me your word?"

"Of course!" Alexia threw her arms around Belial and hugged him fiercely. He tensed and patted her back stiffly as if she were a dog. "Enough of this for now," he said awkwardly. "I will have a servant take you to him. But first I must show you something. It will only take a few minutes." This time the smile did reach his eyes.

Six years earlier

Alexia allowed herself a small smile. She'd picked the roof at Fibber McGees because it gave her the best view of Belfast's market district. It was midday and the market was full to bursting.

The market didn't have a roof, only a wooden framework of beams dividing the merchant stalls. Thick vines and crawling plants wound up wooden posts and sprawled across the beams, offering shade to the shoppers below.

You could buy absolutely anything in the market, from horses to honey, from pastry to pots and pans. The market covered two acres and was never empty.

Perfect, Alexia thought as she hopped from the roof onto the beams that crisscrossed the market. Her crimson cloak spread out behind her as she ran, making her feel like she was flying. Alexia moved quickly, easily keeping her balance. At the very center of the market, the wooden framework fell away. A thick post stood impressively tall, and the sprawling vines rose upward, forming a canopy, like a large tent.

Alexia carefully stepped from her beam and tested the vines. They felt solid enough, so she put her full weight on them and climbed upward. As she reached the top of the canopy, she pushed the vines aside and wriggled her body through so she was hanging upside down.

Hundreds of men, women, and children shopped just a few spans below without ever noticing the girl hanging above them. She giggled, then scanned the crowd and spotted Josiah near one of the bakers' stalls. He was perfectly positioned.

A short distance away, Juno stood close to an older woman who was buying a pendant at one of the jewelers' shops. Juno wore a fancy dress she'd stolen the day before so she wouldn't look like an urchin. She'd even combed her hair and taken a bath for the occasion. The shopkeeper would probably think her the daughter of one of his customers.

Benaiah was a master at concealing himself. It took Alexia a minute before she spotted him hunched in the shadows of the butcher's shop. Summer was stationed near the fruit stall, and Adeline lurked next to the blanket seller. All of Alexia's Gang of Rogues stood ready, awaiting her signal.

Alexia smiled. Even if Korah and his Gang of Terror were trying to capture her, she hadn't been this happy in years. She couldn't remember the last time she'd had a friend.

It's time! She dropped her arms to let them dangle. "Help!" Alexia shrieked. "Please help me!" she cried.

Men and women looked up and began pointing and shouting. Alexia unhooked one of her legs and dropped a bit more, catching the vines above with her ankle and twisting her foot so she wouldn't fall. "Please help me!" she screamed.

Men ran beneath, cradling arms as if to catch her. Women shrieked, "Someone help that poor girl!" As she hung upside down, Alexia turned slowly, scanning the market. Every member of her gang was working. Juno was stuffing necklaces into her satchel, and Josiah was already retreating with a bag filled to bursting with bread. Benaiah was leading three goats through the crowd, and Summer's and Addie's arms were filled to overflowing. All of the shopkeepers were focused on the girl hanging above them.

Alexia yanked a vine free and straightened her leg. She dropped like a stone, savoring every gasp from the crowd below. As the vine went taut and swung her into the pole, the crowd gasped again. Alexia quickly shimmied back to the top and began to laugh. The gasps turned to confused cries as the watchers realized something was amiss.

"It's the girl from the posters!" a woman shouted.

"It's the one they're offering the reward for!" a young man yelled.

"Get her!" another man screamed.

Just that quickly, the crowd of concerned bystanders transformed into an angry mob. Alexia wriggled through the vines and ran down the canopy.

"I've been robbed!" the jeweler shouted.

"Me too!" screamed the baker.

Alexia was so frantic that she placed a foot wrong and fell through the vines, catching herself at the waist. Her legs dangled within reach of her pursuers, but she quickly pulled herself up and leaped for the wooden beams.

She sprinted toward the rooftop of Fibber McGees. But the people below had seen where she was headed, and a few of the men were climbing the wooden structure to try to block her.

Alexia ran even faster, leaping over the head of a man who appeared beneath. She landed on the roof of the large pub and darted up its steep peak, not slowing for a second. And as she raced back to her hideout to meet her friends, Alexia's heart tried to beat out of her chest. *That was too close!*

When Alexia arrived, the others were already there. Her jaw dropped as she reviewed their impressive pile of loot. The heist was a success! Juno had fifteen pendants, four bracelets, and a number of earrings. Josiah upended a bag of bread, while Benaiah grinned as he showed Alexia the three goats and two chickens he'd managed to steal. Adeline unfurled six thick blankets as Summer offered Alexia an apple from her basket of fruit.

Alexia laughed as the children whooped and hollered, dancing about like wild banshees.

Chapter 16

A MOMENT WITH TIME

Jack swam the last strokes toward the tiny island in absolute darkness. The log cabin covered every last inch of the island, so he barely had room to stand on the stoop.

This is it. I came all this way to enter this cabin! He wondered if he should knock. He didn't want to be rude. Taking a deep breath, he knocked loudly on the wooden door and waited.

"Who is it?" A child's voice giggled from inside.

"It's me, Jack Staples," Jack said, trying to sound natural. "May I come in?"

"Of course, silly!" the child replied. "You answered the riddle, didn't you?"

Jack pushed on the door. Inside a fire burned in a hearth that took up an entire wall. Curled up in a large padded chair was a little girl, grinning widely.

"Can you hear it?" she said, giggling as she pulled her feet beneath her. "It's quite wondrous. Please say you can hear it!"

The girl couldn't have been older than five, and her emerald eyes sparkled. She had curly auburn hair and olive skin, and her voice had a dreamlike quality to it.

"Hear what?" Jack asked.

"Your note, of course!" She was wide-eyed with excitement. "It's so beautiful I can barely stand it." She giggled again.

"I can't hear anything," Jack said. "Who are you? I'm here to meet with Time. Do you know her?"

"Yes, I know her." The girl smiled mischievously. "You are funny! I like you a lot. I'm glad the guardians didn't eat you."

"That makes two of us," Jack said. He didn't know why, but this child annoyed him. "Where is Time?" He glanced around the small cabin. They were the only people inside. "Can you take me to her?"

"Of course I can. But first I want to show you something."

"I don't have time," Jack complained. "My friends are waiting, and they need me to hurry."

The little girl laughed so hard she almost fell out of her chair. "You're so funny!" she cried, slapping her palms against the armrests. "Why are you always in such a hurry to be somewhere else?" she asked. "Isn't it more fun to be right where you are?"

Jack ignored her, taking in the tiny cabin. "Why do they call this the Forbidden Garden? It's just a room. You don't even have a plant in here."

The little girl jumped up and smoothed out her frilly blue dress. "You'll need to run fast so the fire doesn't burn you!"

"What are you talking about?"

The girl winked, then darted into the fireplace and disappeared through the back wall.

"Wait!" Jack called after her. "Come back!" He stared at the fireplace, dumbfounded. She obviously wanted him to follow. He waited a moment, sighed irritably, then closed his eyes and screamed as he sprinted into the fire. There was a flash of heat and he braced himself to hit the back wall. But the flames didn't burn, and there was no wall. Jack staggered to a stop and opened his eyes.

Wherever he was, it was daytime and it was extraordinary. Rolling hills of lush grass went on for as far as he could see. He was surrounded by wildflowers, and when he walked, the flowers moved aside so he wouldn't crush them. The place was utterly wild, but at the same time it looked as if every flower, plant, and tree was exactly where it was meant to be. The sky was impossibly blue and the air so clean his lungs almost burned to breathe it.

The little girl was in front of him, standing on her toes. "Do you like it?" she said, sounding both nervous and hopeful.

"It's amazing!" Jack was breathless. "Where are we?"

"We're in the garden, of course!" the girl said happily.

"This is the Forbidden Garden?" Jack asked.

"You aren't forbidden anymore, silly! You are here. So it's just the garden now!"

Jack stared at the rolling hills. It was perfect.

"Can you hear it now?" the girl asked.

"I can't hear anything," Jack said self-consciously.

"It's so beautiful! How do you make it?"

"I don't know what you're talking about, but I can't hear anything. I just need to meet with Time so I can get back to my friends. They need my help."

"I know!" The little girl nodded. "Especially Alexia; she needs you more than ever—you and Arthur and Mrs. Dumphry and all of them! I'm really afraid for her, Jack."

"How do you know about Alexia?" Jack asked. "How do you know about any of them?"

"Look." The girl pointed at the sky. Jack looked up and the sky became a swirl of colors. As he watched, Alexia appeared in the colors.

Jack gasped. Alexia was with the Assassin and she was … hugging him! They were standing in a room of shadows and monsters. Jack wanted to ask the little girl what he was seeing, but the sky changed. Arthur Greaves was alone on an empty street in a city of shadows. He was wearing a black-and-silver cloak and he was … dancing!

Next, the sky revealed a battle … *No*, Jack thought, *it's hundreds of battles, thousands of them!* The entire world was at war; every tree, every blade of grass, every creature and human fought for survival. Mountains trembled as oceans boiled and stars fell from the sky. The Awakened fought dark servants, and at first Jack thought the Awakened might be winning. But then something exploded and a shadow ripped across the sky. Within seconds all the earth was covered in darkness and there were no more images to see.

Jack stared at the sky for a long time, trying to understand. When he finally tore his eyes away, he saw the little girl sitting on an ocean of wildflowers, watching the sky with a look of immense sadness.

"Was that the future?" Jack asked. "Was that what's going to happen?"

"It was a future," she said sadly. "The story is still being written, but unless we can help Alexia, it is the most likely ending, I think."

Jack sat beside her and spoke without thinking. "You are Time."

The girl leaned forward. "I am!" she said. "Everyone always thinks they will meet someone who looks older than Mrs. Dumphry! Isn't that crazy?" She laughed. "Why would I be old? What a funny thought!" She bounced up, turned, and ran. Somehow the shifting wildflowers seemed natural in this place.

"Wait!" Jack yelled. "Where are you going?"

"I need to take you somewhere, silly!" Time called. "Follow me!"

Jack chased after her. The earth and sky, the air itself radiated energy, each breath flooding him with life. It was hard to stay depressed in a place like this. *I know this place!* Jack realized. *It feels the same as when I went through the Masc Tinneas and saw the Assassin singing that song. The land and air are the same!*

Jack didn't grow tired as he ran; each step brought more energy. He began to laugh as he ran even faster. Time had disappeared into a small copse of trees, and as Jack darted in, he skidded to a stop, almost knocking her over. Time stood beside a small pond.

"Can you hear it now?" she asked.

Jack stopped and listened. He was surprised to find he wasn't breathing heavily at all. "I can't—" Jack stopped. He did hear something. It was the ringing of a single note. It was faint, but coming from somewhere nearby. "What is it?" he whispered.

"It's your note!" Time whispered back, her emerald eyes sparkling with delight.

"What do you mean?"

"Everyone has a note," Time said, seriously. "This is yours. No one else can make this sound but you. Isn't it wonderful?"

"It is." The music grew stronger as he listened. It was a single note, but it sounded like a symphony. "This is the ringing I hear each time I go back," he said. "It's what takes me back in time!"

"Yes," Time said, "that's right! Your note is very special, Jack. It's one of my favorites! And when you are both together, I can barely stand it!"

"You mean … when I am with Alexia?"

"Yes! When you are together, I feel as if nothing bad can happen!" Time giggled again.

"I don't know about that," Jack said. "Plenty of bad has happened since we've been together. My mother—" Jack stopped.

"Your mother gave her life to save you. There is no greater gift," Time said.

"But she's still gone."

"She's not gone, silly. I see her standing before me now. She lives in you and she lives in Alexia. And death is not the end. It's the start of the grandest adventure yet!"

"She lives in Alexia?"

"Well, why wouldn't she?" Time shook her head. "Alexia is your sister, after all."

"What do you mean she's my sister?"

"I mean you both have the same parents, silly! What else would I mean?" Time giggled. "And when you're both together, your notes are so beautiful they make me want to cry."

"That doesn't make sense!" Jack insisted. "Parker is my brother. I only met Alexia recently."

"Parker Dreager is your adopted brother." Time sounded as though she were explaining something completely obvious. "Alexia and Parker were switched so the Assassin wouldn't find her. Parker is the son of Madeleine and Caleb Dreager."

Jack sat down. He was dizzy as he tried to make sense of it. But it did make sense. When Jack had gone back in time, he'd seen his mother holding a baby girl. It must have been Alexia.

"Are you ready to leave the garden now?" Time extended a hand, waiting for Jack to take it.

"You want me to leave? I just got here." Jack didn't want to go back to his world just yet. He felt safer here than he'd felt in a long time.

"I'm going with you, silly!" Time said. "I have to show you something."

Jack took her hand and inhaled deeply, filling his lungs with pure energy.

"Are you ready?" Time asked again, and Jack nodded. "Okay, then, all you need to do is listen for your note and when you hear it, embrace it!"

"How do you embrace a sound?"

"Until now, every time you've heard it, you've tried to make it do what you wanted. But that's not right. Your note comes from the Author. It is what defines you. When you embrace it, you let it decide where to take you. You needn't worry about going to the wrong place or time if you let the Author decide."

Jack shook his head. "Who is this Author everyone keeps talking about? And what do you mean—he gave me my note?"

"That's what you're here to see, of course! Take my hand and I'll show you."

As Jack took hold of Time's hand, the bells inside his chest rose to a symphony. Jack and Time lurched backward, flying through the air.

"Before you go see your friend beneath the coliseum," Belial said to Alexia, "I want to show you something." He reached around his neck and grabbed a thin chain. At the end of the chain was a small stone, streaked through with blue veins. It was exactly the same as the one Alexia had taken from her father's chamber. The blue veins glowed with a flickering light.

"My lady," Belial said, "this is a Memory Stone. It captures the memories of anyone who wears it. And before you go and talk with your friend, I wish to show you one of my memories. Hold it tightly in your fist and close your eyes." Belial handed Alexia the stone.

Alexia clenched her hand around it as the stone began to warm. When Belial wrapped his hands around hers, blue light shone faintly from between their fingers.

"Show us the poet's death," Belial whispered.

The last thing in the world Alexia wanted to see was Belial killing a man, but before she could say a word, the world shifted around her.

Alexia gasped. They were still in the throne room, but it had changed. Everything looked newer and somehow more real. She had become used to the otherworldly feeling of Thaltorose over the weeks, but in the memory the throne room was far more substantial and there were no shadows slithering in the corners.

"Are we still in Thaltorose?" Alexia asked, letting go of Belial's hand.

"Yes. Though the city used to have a different name. This particular memory is more than five thousand years old."

Five thousand years!

The throne room was completely still, as if the memory hadn't started yet. It was far better lit than Alexia was used to, with torches and fire pits, though not a single flame moved. Alexia and Belial stood near the center of a crowd of hundreds who had gathered.

Alexia turned to see a beautiful red-haired woman in an elaborate dress of silver and ruby thread. She was sitting on a large golden throne encrusted in rubies, though it didn't come close to the size of Belial's throne. Mirrors of every size surrounded all but the front of the throne, so the red-haired woman could view herself from every angle.

She must be the queen, Alexia realized. Behind the queen, two men in white and silver cloaks stood in the shadows with heads bowed. Standing before the queen was a man in a colorful patchwork cloak.

"This is the poet I told you about." Flames raged in Belial's eyes. He waved a hand and the memory lurched into motion.

Chapter 17

THE DEATH OF THE AUTHOR

Five thousand and twenty-four years earlier

Jack blinked. He still held Time's hand, but they were no longer in the garden. They stood in the middle of an enormous hall filled with torches and blazing hearths. They were surrounded by a large crowd of men and women who were dressed in layered silks. Jack looked down and was shocked to see that he and Time wore the same kind of lavish garments as everyone else.

The hall was enormous. The floor was smooth marble, and looming large in the center was a golden throne inlaid with rubies and surrounded by mirrors. A beautiful red-haired woman, wearing a dress of silver and ruby, sat on the throne.

"That is the queen." Time stood on tiptoe as she whispered into Jack's ear.

"Where are we?" he whispered. "And when are we?"

When Time looked at him, she didn't smile and she didn't giggle. "We have gone back more than five thousand years," she said. "This is the worst day ever. I hate it! But you need to see what happened if you are going to save the world." Time pushed her way through the crowd, pulling Jack until they stood at the front of the gathering.

Two men stood in the shadows behind the throne, wearing cloaks of white and silver, but all of Jack's attention was given to the fire-haired queen. She sat on her throne studying a man who stood before her. He wore a colorful patchwork cloak and did not look afraid. He had kind eyes, and though Jack was sure he'd never seen him before, the man seemed very familiar.

"You dare speak against me?" the queen said. "You are here to answer for your crimes, yet you dig yourself ever deeper." Even as she talked, her eyes drifted to the mirrors and she watched herself.

"My queen"—one of the men behind the throne stepped forward—"if I may speak?"

Jack gasped. It was the Assassin. He looked different than he did now, more human, but Jack was sure it was him. He wore a cloak of white and silver.

"It's you!" Alexia whispered to Belial.

"Yes," he said with a smile. "But you needn't whisper, my lady. They cannot see or hear you. This is only a memory."

Alexia studied the younger Belial from the memory. He looked the same, yet also different. There was something … more human about him. And he was quite handsome!

"My queen"—the memory of Belial stepped forward—"if I may speak?"

"Speak," the queen said.

"As your chief adviser, I must tell you I believe this poet to be the most dangerous man your kingdom has ever seen. He calls himself a simple poet, but he has enticed your people with honeyed words. And if you do not act now, your kingdom will fall."

The queen barked a laugh as she turned to study herself in a mirror. She rearranged her garments as she spoke. "You give this poet far too much credit. Would you have me rid the kingdom of every bard and sonneteer? Would you have me throw every storyteller in chains?"

"I would, Your Majesty," the humanlike Belial said. "But this man is the most dangerous of them all. I believe you should make an example of him. I believe this … poet," he sneered, "should be killed without delay."

The poet watched the queen, but he didn't look upset in the least. There was something peaceful about his eyes. Something about the man made Alexia feel ... good. She couldn't say why, but she liked him immediately.

"No!" said the second man who had been standing behind the throne. He stepped forward and bowed low. "Forgive me, Your Majesty, but I cannot stand aside and listen to this."

"What?" Alexia was suddenly dizzy. She knew the man.

"I don't understand!" Jack whispered. "That's Aias! It's not possible!" Aias looked much as he had the last time Jack had seen him, except he still had both arms and didn't have the scar crossing through his right eye and down his chin.

Time didn't answer. She just squeezed Jack's hand as she watched the human-looking Belial with horror painting her face.

"I agree that this man is not just a simple poet," Aias said carefully. "His words are revolutionary, but I do not think they will bring destruction. Hear this poet for yourself, Your Majesty. Let him speak freely, then decide what you must do with him."

"You cannot allow him to speak." Belial spoke to the queen but looked at Aias. "You must not! He will destroy it all! You must do as I say and kill him now!"

The queen held up a hand to silence the men. She was too busy preening to see the dangerous look in Belial's eyes.

"I will allow him to speak." The queen turned to the man. "But I warn you, poet. I am tempted to end your life and be done with it."

Jack stepped forward, breaking from the crowd of onlookers. Something about the queen was familiar. Time grasped his hand and pulled him back. "Please don't leave me," she whispered. "I don't want to be alone. It's going to happen soon and I'm scared!"

"What's going to happen?" Jack whispered. But Time didn't answer. Her whole body trembled as she watched the Assassin.

Alexia studied the poet's face. *How can I be so drawn to a man I've never met before?* It was a peculiar thought. The man didn't look afraid in the slightest. Alexia's breath caught as the poet stared directly at her. *It's not possible!* she thought. *It's just a memory.* The poet held her gaze a moment longer, then winked before turning his attention back to the queen. As he stepped forward, he pulled a small harp from his cloak and began to strum.

The poet met the queen's eyes and spoke with a quiet authority, his fingers strumming a tune to accompany his words. "There once was a queen so powerful that she had conquered the entire world." The poet's voice carried clearly throughout the mammoth chamber. "She ruled over every man, woman, and child on earth. In fact, so powerful was this queen that even the beasts of the field and the birds of the air were subject to her."

The poet's fingers moved along the harp, playing a haunting tune.

Alexia's chest tightened. She knew the end of this story; Belial had told her. This poet was about to die. *How could anyone hate this man?*

"There was nothing this queen did not rule over." The poet's voice was captivating. "But still, she felt empty inside." He plucked a string, making it warble like the cry of a hungry bird. "The queen had absolute power and riches beyond measure. Anything she wanted was hers, but there was no joy in her heart."

Alexia listened to his words. There was something very meaningful about his story. She had the distinct feeling the story was not just for the queen, but for her as well.

"And though the queen ruled the world, she was not a wise woman," the poet continued. "For this queen believed power was found in control. One day she left her castle and went for a walk, and she heard laughter from somewhere deep in the woods. Yet she did not recognize it. You see, the queen had not heard laughter in her kingdom for so many years she'd forgotten its sound." The poet's fingers plucked a sorrowful tune.

"She followed the laughter until she found its source. Two children were playing together beside a river. They sang songs and danced with abandon. They told stories and laughed till their bellies ached!" The poet's strumming had become momentarily playful.

"As the queen watched, she became jealous of the children. Her jealousy quickly turned to rage. For she realized these two children were far more powerful than she had ever been."

Alexia wanted to shout at the man. She wanted to tell him to stop speaking. The queen had turned her attention from the mirrors and was watching him with a dangerous look in her eyes. But the poet was facing the crowd.

Alexia squinted at the queen. The fire-haired woman suddenly reminded her of someone. She stepped closer.

As Jack listened to the poet, Time squeezed his hand all the harder. Something bad was going to happen. He could feel it.

"The queen watched the children playing and laughing, and she hated them." The poet's plucking song held the feeling of impending doom. "You see, every child understands that true power, true freedom can only come from surrender."

The poet met Jack's eyes and smiled. "Enraged at the children's freedom, at their immense power, the queen could take it no longer. She ran out from behind her tree and drowned both children in the river." The poet's plucking stopped dead as the last note echoed through the chamber.

The gathered crowd gasped at the horrific twist to the tale. Time stiffened and began whispering under her breath. "I hate this part! I hate this part! I hate this part!" She trembled as tears streamed down her face.

The poet turned to the queen. "You see, what your adviser has told you is true. I have been telling a different story. There is a new way to live, a way filled with joy and laughter and music and dancing." The poet smiled. "It's the way of love; it is the way of a child; and it is far more powerful than anything you have known. And this new way of living is available to you as well."

"You dare speak to me this way?" The queen shook with rage.

The poet stepped forward and cupped the queen's chin with his hand. "Love in the place of jealousy, wisdom in the place of pride, humility in the place of vanity." His words were clear and strong.

The queen was so taken aback that for a moment she didn't move, but just stood there, gazing into his eyes. As the poet stepped away, the queen shook her head. Aias stepped forward and placed a hand on her shoulder. "Please, my queen, do not act hastily!"

The queen snatched a golden knife from her belt and screamed as she whipped around and struck out. Aias groaned as he fell back, clutching his ruined eye as blood spurted from the wound.

Jack felt like someone had punched him in the stomach. He knew who the queen was. "It's not possible!" he whispered.

"Mrs. Dumphry!" Alexia exclaimed. "It can't be!" The longer she looked at the queen, the more sure she became.

The humanlike Belial stepped forward and placed his hands on the queen's shoulders, speaking quietly, though Alexia was close enough to hear.

"If you do not make an example of this poet, his words will spread like wildfire and your kingdom will fall. But if you kill him now, all the power he possesses will be yours!"

The queen shook her head as she looked at the poet. "I don't … I can't. Maybe he's right?"

The Assassin's eyes blazed. "He has deceived you! The only way to break his spell is to kill him. Do it now!"

The queen nodded grimly as she stepped forward and plunged the golden dagger into the poet's side. The great hall erupted as men and women screamed in horror. Aias cried out, "No!" But the act was already done. Behind the queen, a look of ecstasy entered Belial's eyes.

Alexia felt the real Belial grab her hand. In the horror of the moment, she'd forgotten she was in a memory. Just before the world shifted around her, Alexia saw Jack Staples in the crowd. He was standing next to a very strange little girl.

Chapter 18

BIRTH OF THE SHADOWFOG

Present day

Arthur was terrified. He stood behind a large boulder on the outskirts of a City of Shadows. Mrs. Dumphry, Aias, and Andreal were nearby. It had taken the small band more than two weeks to journey to Thaltorose. The World Portal had spit them into a desolate land of black stone and scorching white sand. They'd had to walk from there, and each day had been fraught with danger.

On three separate occasions they'd been ambushed and forced to run, barely escaping with their lives. Arthur nearly had his head taken off by a creature that was more bird than human. The creature's winged arms had been razor sharp, and it wielded them with the skill of a Blades Master.

The only way they'd made it safely to the outskirts of the shadowed city was by ambushing a band of dark servants. They'd stolen four of the filthy black-and-silver uniforms and put them on, pretending to belong to the Assassin's army. It had been the most traumatizing two weeks of Arthur's young life.

He peeked around the boulder to stare at the city once again. It was a place of nightmares. The sky was an otherworldly yellow, and a swirl of dark clouds floated far above. *Those aren't clouds*, Arthur thought as he gazed upward. *The swirling darkness is alive!* Tens of thousands of winged creatures circled above the city.

Arthur wanted to look away, to run, but he couldn't tear his eyes from the horrific scene. Hundreds of twisting black spires rose throughout the city; standing boldly at the center was a monstrous palace that shone with eerie light.

Arthur squeezed his eyes shut and turned his attention back to Mrs. Dumphry and the others. They were huddled under the overhang of a large black bolder, discussing the best way to enter the city. When Arthur saw the look in Mrs. Dumphry's eyes, his heart sank even further.

She's afraid, he realized. It made him feel more terrified than ever. He'd seen his teacher face impossible odds, but he had never seen her look like this before.

"Mrs. Dumphry," Arthur interrupted, "can we really save Alexia?"

Mrs. Dumphry turned to look at the city. When she spoke, her voice was grave. "I do not know, child, but we must try. If we fail, the war will be lost and the entire world will become like this city. It will be a world of shadows and monsters."

"I don't understand!" Alexia pleaded. "What just happened? Was that really Mrs. Dumphry?"

"Yes," Belial said, "it was." He offered a hand and waited until Alexia took it. Together they walked toward one of the many exits of the throne room. "I needed you to see the truth, my lady. I needed you to understand the unfairness of it all."

Belial turned and knelt before Alexia. "The woman you know as Mrs. Dumphry used to be the queen of this city, and her rule extended over much of the world. And as you saw, I was her most trusted adviser. Though it was she who killed the poet with her own hands, they named me Assassin."

Alexia didn't care who had killed the poet; she just hated that he'd been killed. He had seemed so kind. "Wait." Alexia stopped. "I thought they named you Assassin because you killed someone they call the Author?"

Belial shook his head sadly. "The poet and the Author are one and the same, my lady. They are but two names for the same man."

"I don't understand! Aren't the Awakened following this Author person? Isn't he their leader?"

"Yes," Belial said. "Now you know the whole truth. They follow a poet who died thousands of years ago. What's worse is that Mrs.

Dumphry is one of their leaders. And you saw her kill the man with your own eyes."

It doesn't make sense! But she had seen it. Even if she wished Belial hadn't told Mrs. Dumphry to kill the poet, the man was dead. And who would follow a dead man?

"We are done for today," Belial said. "If you still wish to go and see those who stand against us, those you name as your friends, then go. But remember what you saw. And remember that you have promised to follow me in all things."

Alexia nodded. As she walked from the throne room, she felt sick to her stomach.

Five thousand and twenty-four years earlier

Jack watched the horrific scene play out in front of him. The queen, the much younger Mrs. Dumphry, pulled her golden knife from the poet's side and dropped it to the floor. Behind her, the Assassin let out a bloodcurdling laugh. As the blood of the poet dripped onto the marble, the queen sank to her knees in front of him.

"*No,*" she said shakily. "What have I done? Please forgive me!"

The gathered crowd shrieked as they fled the throne room. Time was screaming at the top of her lungs as tears streamed down her face. Jack couldn't tear his eyes away from the poet in the patchwork cloak. He had dropped to his knees and was holding a hand to the wound in his side. He reached out with his free hand and placed it on the side of the queen's face, then whispered something Jack couldn't hear. Whatever he said caused the queen to gasp and weep all the harder.

Throughout the chamber the fires began to extinguish themselves as the room decayed into darkness. Yet it was only dark for a moment. At the center of the chamber, a shadowed light began to pulse. It was faint at first, but grew brighter with each surge. *The light is coming from the Assassin*, Jack realized.

The pulsing darkness revealed the Assassin in all his glory. His humanness was gone and he had been transformed into the creature Jack had seen many times before. His eyes were caverns of fire and his skin sparkled like diamonds.

The poet still lived but had lost much blood. He was incredibly pale, lying on his back on the marble floor. The queen knelt beside him, weeping.

Only Jack and Time remained. Time was no longer screaming, but stood stiffly by his side, weeping. Jack scooped her into his arms and carried her behind a nearby pillar. When he looked again, he saw the Assassin standing over the poet.

"Was this the best you could do?" the Assassin snarled. "Before this world was born, you brought a child to the Sacred Mountain. You told me the child would destroy me." The Assassin raised his fist. "But what child could stand against me when the most powerful queen willingly does my bidding? You have lost! I have turned the humans against you! Do you hear? I have already won!"

The queen was on her knees, watching the Assassin with a look of horror. Aias ignored the gaping wound on his face. Moving like a viper, he drew his black sword and leaped at the Assassin. Jack recognized the blade. It was Ashandar, the same sword now buckled at Jack's waist. Aias screamed as he swung Ashandar with all his might.

The blade ricocheted off the Assassin's neck as if Aias had struck stone.

The Assassin turned to face a stunned Aias. "You are a worm standing before a god," he rasped as liquid evil exploded into Aias's chest and sent him flying into the darkness. When the Assassin turned to face the queen, he offered a cold smile.

"You have done well," he said. "Bow before me now and I will spare your life. Prostrate yourself and swear to serve me always, and I will give you more power than you have ever known!"

The queen's eyes stayed locked on the poet as she stood. The pool of blood he was lying in was growing larger by the second. "I don't understand," she said. "Who was he really? And why did you tell me to kill him?"

"In Siyyon, the world where I was born, we called him Author," the Assassin said. "I suppose you could say he was my father, that he was the father of all worlds." The Assassin knelt beside the dying poet and rummaged through his patchwork cloak, pulling out a carved wooden box and a shiny feathered pen.

"One day, I was walking along the Great River near the Sacred Mountain." The Assassin twisted the wooden box as he spoke. "And when I bent down to drink, I saw my reflection. In that moment I realized something. The Author was not all-powerful as I had supposed. He could not possibly be! For what being would create something more majestic than itself? And in that moment I decided in my heart to kill him."

Jack heard a click as the Assassin twisted the box again and a small hole appeared in the top. He stuck the feathered pen into the hole, and as it went inside, it acted as a key, opening a door in the top of the box. Jack couldn't see if anything was inside.

The Assassin screamed and slammed his fist hard against the Author's chest. The Author gasped as his body jerked violently. With ravenous eyes, the Assassin bent low and whispered in his ear.

Jack couldn't hear what the Assassin said, but he recognized the box. When he'd looked into the strange map—the Masc Tinneas—in the schoolhouse in Ballylesson, Jack had seen Parker and his father running from a vast darkness, Parker clutching the box as he ran.

The Assassin rose triumphantly. He placed the box inside his cloak and dropped the feathered pen. He stared down at the poet's dead body and began to laugh. The laugh grew louder and louder. "IT IS FINISHED!" he screamed, throwing his arms wide.

The Assassin's words echoed through the throne room, and hundreds of dark tendrils rose from the marble floor. They slithered upward to swirl around the Assassin's feet, thickening into larger tentacles.

"The Shadowfog," Jack whispered.

"THE AUTHOR IS DEAD!" the Assassin screamed. "TAKE THE CITY!" The Shadowfog blanketed the floor, forming an ocean of darkness as it flowed from the chamber and into the palace.

The screaming started almost immediately. Hundreds of people, thousands of them, shrieking and wailing as the Shadowfog rushed over them and out into the streets.

The Assassin knelt beside the poet's body and placed a large vial on the marble floor.

"Rathule Magasulem!" He pointed at the pool of blood surrounding the poet. The blood began to ripple as it came together. "Radakcha!" He pointed at the vial and the blood flowed inside. Careful not to touch the top, the Assassin snatched the bottle and corked it, then placed it carefully inside his cloak.

When he stood to face the queen, a dangerous light shone in his eyes. "Bow before me," he said. "Vow to serve me always and I will give you a seat at my right hand."

Chapter 19

A DIMMING LIGHT

Six years earlier

Only one day after the successful pilfering of Belfast's central market, Alexia and her Gang of Rogues were back. This time their mission was far simpler—to steal a little hay and grain to feed the animals they'd taken the day before.

As they walked to the market, Alexia had been proud to see her "Wanted" poster stuck to every lamppost. Each time she saw her face on a poster, she smiled. It made her feel important and dangerous.

Someone inside the market started to scream. Alexia and her friends rose on tiptoes to see what was happening, but they were too short. There were more screams—something was happening on the other side of the market and people began to flee.

Josiah didn't hesitate. While the shopkeeper's attention was turned to the screams, he grabbed a large bale of hay from a nearby stall. Benaiah stole a bucket of grain. Both boys turned and walked quickly in the direction of a nearby alley. One by one the others also stole some hay or grain and slipped away. Alexia hesitated; whatever was happening had piqued her curiosity.

"We got what we came for!" Juno tugged her sleeve. "Let's go before someone catches us!"

Alexia shook her head. "I'm going to stay. You take the others back to the hideout. I'll join you in a few minutes. I want to see what's going on!"

Juno rolled her eyes before disappearing into the alley. Alexia darted toward the center of the market. All around her, men, women, and children sprinted in the opposite direction. It was chaos like nothing she'd seen before. Shopkeepers abandoned their wares and fled. Every last person was desperate to escape what was coming.

Alexia climbed onto a shopkeeper's table to get a better look. What she saw took her breath away—a large elephant pulling a covered wagon was galloping through the packed marketplace. And Alexia was the only one not screaming.

Excitement shone in her eyes as the mammoth beast galloped toward her, destroying everything in its path. Fruit and vegetable stands went flying, and hanging slabs of meat dropped to the dusty ground. Stalls filled with clothing, lamps, glassware, candles, chickens, goats, pastries, and almost everything imaginable were smashed aside by the elephant and the wagon. The elephant's eyes were rolled back, showing only the whites.

What on earth is an elephant doing here? She hadn't been this excited since the day she'd learned how to skin a rabbit with one hand. Alexia had always had a way with animals. Whether wild or tame, they seemed to like her. So she had no doubt this elephant would be the same. She threw her crimson cloak over her shoulders and fully extended one arm with palm outstretched.

"Ha!" she yelled as loudly as she could. "Stop right there!"

If anything, the elephant sped up slightly.

"I said, Stop!" Alexia screamed as fear threatened to overcome her excitement. And still the beast crashed ever closer.

"Oh, no." But it was too late. Before she could so much as turn around, the elephant was on her. The beast whipped its massive head to the side and slammed a tusk against her body. She felt at least three ribs crack as she hurtled over five stalls to land in the middle of a pigsty.

Bruised and angry, Alexia struggled to stand as she wiped mud from her eyes. When she turned to see where the elephant had gone, she froze. The covered wagon had upended and burst apart.

The stunned elephant and destroyed wagon were not what worried Alexia. It was the two dizzy and agitated lions that were struggling to rise. The beasts had been caged in the back of the wagon and both were now free, watching Alexia with hungry eyes.

The lions were identical except for the color of their manes; one was black and one golden. The golden-maned lion had a fresh cut on its shoulder and a wild look in its eyes. The terrified elephant stood a few paces away, still connected to the upended cart.

Lions and elephants roaming the streets of Belfast! It's not possible!

The black-maned lion roared loudly, baring its teeth. The two beasts were now on opposite sides of Alexia, so she needed to move continuously to keep them in sight. But there was nowhere to go. When the golden lion behind her roared, the black-maned lion attacked.

In sheer panic, she squeezed her eyes shut and clenched her fists, waiting for the beasts to collide with her. Yet besides the sudden burst of wind that ripped at her clothes, there was ... nothing. Ever so slowly Alexia opened her eyes. Both lions were sprawled on the ground on either side of her, lying motionless, as if dead.

"What?" Alexia turned to see the elephant, goats, cows, pigs, and chickens all lying on the ground. Every animal she could see—

They're dead! The thought made her want to cry. *What happened? How could all of them have died at the exact same time?* It was too horrible to imagine. She knelt and placed a hand on the head of the golden-maned lion. As her fingers touched its fur, the mighty beast let out a soft purr.

Alexia screamed as she jumped back. Though she was relieved it was alive, she didn't want to be too close. It was still a lion, after all. The second lion opened its eyes groggily, and when it looked at Alexia, it also began to purr.

After spotting a spool of twine in the wreckage of a nearby shop, Alexia quickly fashioned a leash around each beast's neck while they were still dazed. She took the end of the twine and tied it to the ruined wagon wheel. "There!" She smiled. "That should keep them from eating me."

As the rest of the animals in the marketplace began to move, Alexia walked over to get a better look at the elephant. It was no longer panicked but seemed to be completely at peace. As she approached, an image formed unbidden in her mind—she saw herself standing before the elephant, shining as bright as the sun. The image was so clear it made her stop and gape. She shook her head to clear her thoughts.

A number of men on horseback galloped into the marketplace, led by a man in a royal blue cloak whose clothes were made of hundreds of patches. Not the tattered patches of a poet, though—these patches were the color of gold, silver, copper, and iron, and each sparkled and shimmered as he moved. On the man's head was a ridiculously tall hat.

"What's this, then? What has happened here?" He leaped from his horse. "Who are you, child, and what have you done to my animals?" The man strutted to the lions, inspecting them closely as he pulled on the twine and examined the knots. Next he sauntered to the elephant and peered into its eyes.

"I didn't do anything!" Alexia hated being referred to as a child. "Your elephant nearly trampled the whole market before I stopped it!"

The man turned slowly, taking in the sight of the animals and the destroyed marketplace.

"You ... stopped the elephant?" he asked. "You captured the lions?" He had an astonished look in his eyes as he glanced at her hand resting on the elephant's trunk.

Alexia wasn't sure what happened, but she would not allow this man to accuse her.

"Your lions didn't tie themselves up." She made herself meet his eyes.

The man let out a thunderous laugh. "Girl, my name is Julius Argentine Samuelsson the Third, and I am the circus master of the most spectacular circus on earth. But you may call me Julius."

Alexia stared at the circus master's outstretched hand. She'd not told anyone her real name for more than two years now. "My name is Blade," she said coldly, "and if you call me 'girl' or 'child' again, you will regret it."

The circus master bowed his head respectfully. "Blade, is it? What an interesting and, dare I say, dangerous name."

He cleared his throat. "Well, Blade, if I am not mistaken you are quite the remarkable gir"—he stopped himself and tipped his hat—"quite the remarkable young woman. As we rode in, I saw your picture pinned on half the lampposts in Belfast. But whatever the police want with you is not my concern." The circus master bent low to look her in the eyes. "What would you say if I offered you a job in my circus? You could spend your days with the elephants. You could clean up after them and help me keep them calm."

Alexia didn't know what to say. She'd always dreamed of seeing the circus, and spending time with elephants whenever she wanted was too good to be true! For just a moment she thought of her Gang of Rogues. But Alexia knew she couldn't stay in Belfast, not with Korah still looking for her.

"Agreed," she said, shaking the circus master's hand.

Present day

Alexia shivered as the Shadule led her into the dungeons below the coliseum. The creature didn't seem nearly so evil as it once had. In fact, there was something graceful about the way it moved.

No! Alexia couldn't believe she'd just had the thought. It was a Shadule that had tried to kill her more than once. She'd almost died fighting—and killing—one of them in the battle of Agartha. It had been a Shadule that killed her parents.

Alexia stopped. Her father *wasn't* dead. True, he was nothing like she remembered, but he was alive. Why did she keep thinking of him as if he were dead? She might not like her father very much, but she finally had a family. She could finally belong to someone. It's all she'd wanted since her fifth birthday.

If that's true, why does it feel so terrible? she wondered.

The Shadule stopped and looked back. "Why have you stopped, my lady?"

"No reason," she said quickly. She had stopped in front of a large steel door bound by thick chains and a heavy lock. Over the door was an etching of a singing bird.

"My lady?" the Shadule said again.

She hurried to catch up. "Just take me to the prisoners," she said.

A few minutes later the Shadule unlocked a large iron door and stepped aside. Alexia took a deep breath, lifted her torch high, and entered the dark cell. She was shocked to see not one but five pairs of eyes appear in the torchlight. As she walked in, Alexia heard someone gasp.

"Blade! Is that you?"

More gasps followed as she stepped deeper into the cell. She spotted Josiah immediately; he wore far more bruises than when she'd seen him on the street. And Juno, Benaiah, Summer, and Adeline were all there. Every member of the Gang of Rogues stared at Alexia in disbelief.

"Yes," Alexia said after a moment. "Yes, it's me."

"What on earth are you doing here? And dressed like one of them!" Josiah asked.

"She's with them," Juno said. "Can't you see? She came here with the Shadule."

Alexia turned to see the Shadule standing in the doorway. "No," she said, "or, I guess … I don't know. Maybe I am. But it's not what you think!"

"Blade, what are you thinking?" Benaiah said. "Don't you know what they are?"

"Listen to me." Alexia turned her gaze on Josiah. "Belial told me that you joined the Awakened. Is that true?"

"Yes," Josiah said. "When you didn't come back, we went to the market to look for you. But we found Korah. He was with a Shadule and was also searching. That's when the scales fell off our eyes—when we saw the Shadule. We didn't have a chance. We were all as blind as babes when Korah captured us and brought us here. He's tortured us, Blade! And starved us. At first he was looking for information about you—but when he realized we didn't know anything, he didn't stop. He tortures us now because he likes it."

Alexia felt sick to her stomach. *They came looking for me?* They were her friends and she'd left without a second thought. They had been captured and tortured because they were her friends.

"We've been here for years," Josiah continued. "The other prisoners taught us about the Awakened and the Author. We've seen what these creatures do. They are evil, Blade! How could you be with them?"

Alexia shook her head, trying to dispel the choking guilt. "None of that matters now," she said. "You need to listen to me! I was one of the Awakened for a while, but I was wrong!" She grabbed Josiah's hands. "Belial isn't all that bad. He said he would let you go if you promise to serve us." She looked at the others. "He will let all of you go. You can stay with me and we can have anything we want! Food, clothing, money, it doesn't matter. We can have it all!"

Alexia imagined her entire gang leaping to their feet and cheering for her as they once had, but this time there was no reaction at all. None of them said a word. They just stared as if she'd grown a second head.

"Well, what do you say?" Alexia said. "You can be free! I can take you out of here right now!"

"Blade," Josiah said. "Didn't you hear me? Korah has tortured us. He has starved us."

Alexia felt a small stab in her heart. She squared her shoulders as if getting ready to take a punch. "The thing is …" She didn't know how to continue. "The thing is," she said again, "Lord Korah is my father."

Summer gasped and stepped back. Benaiah wrapped Adeline in a hug. Josiah just shook his head.

"I told you, didn't I?" Juno said bitterly. "She left without a word. She promised to join us … to lead us, and then she left without even saying good-bye. She's not who you think she is, Josiah. She never was."

Each word made Alexia's chest tighten. She didn't know what to say. She could barely stand to look at her friends. She tried again, desperate to make them see. "You must listen to me! Belial will let you go! All you need to do is follow us; it's all he asks."

"Follow … us?" Josiah sat down, his disbelief crumbling into disgust.

Alexia realized it might not be the best time to describe her new role as High Princess of Thaltorose. "Never mind that now," she said. "I bet you think the Awakened are good, don't you? But I bet you don't know it wasn't Belial who killed your stupid Author; it was one of your own. You must listen to me. If you knew the things I knew, if you'd seen what I've seen, you'd follow him too!"

Juno stepped forward until she stood nose to nose with Alexia. "I think it's time for you to go," she said dangerously. "Run along and tell the Assassin we will not bow. All the food and clothes and money in the world won't make a difference." She turned her back on Alexia and walked back to stand next to Josiah. "Oh," she said over her shoulder, "and don't forget to give Daddy a hug when you see him."

"Fine!" Alexia said. "But when he hurts you, remember you could have been saved if you hadn't been too proud to bow."

As she stomped from the cell, something died inside Alexia, as if a dim light had faded into darkness. She hated what just happened, but what could she do? As the Shadule led her down the dank passageway, she heard Benaiah call out, "It's not pride that keeps us from bowing; it's hope."

Outside the dungeon, Alexia breathed deeply. She was no longer afraid. She had accepted her position as High Princess of Thaltorose. It was time she stopped behaving like a child. If people chose to follow a dead poet, how could she be expected to stop them?

They deserve what's coming to them, she thought bitterly. Though she wasn't sure she believed it, she wrapped the thought tightly around her heart.

Chapter 20

WHEN EYES ARE OPENED

The City of Shadows was unlike anything Arthur had imagined. A putrid stink emanated from every stone, and the air burned Arthur's lungs. The entire city felt somehow … flimsy or intangible. Whenever Arthur looked directly at something, it seemed completely real, but the world at the corners of his vision darkened slightly, as if it were only a shadow of the real world.

The humans in the city wore necklaces of gold and gemstones. And though their clothes were colorful, their skin was gray and their eyes lifeless. The creatures and monsters were even sicklier than the humans.

182 MARK BATTERSON and JOEL N. CLARK

Everywhere he looked were slithering shadows crawling over walls and streets. They weren't real, or if they were, they had no bodies. They were the shadows of something unseen. In the sky above, thousands of monsters flew—so many that it often looked like one solid mass.

Arthur, Mrs. Dumphry, Aias, and Andreal marched through the city draped in their stolen cloaks of black and silver. So far they had been able to pass themselves off as members of the Shadow Army. When they'd entered the city gates more than two hours earlier, a Drogule had eyed them closely, especially Mrs. Dumphry, but in the end it hadn't tried to stop them.

"How do you know where to go?" Arthur whispered as they walked. "I would have been lost ages ago." Arthur was relatively certain they were walking toward a massive palace at the center of the city, but there were so many twists and turns he was completely turned about.

"This was once the most powerful city on earth," Mrs. Dumphry said. "Thousands of years ago a vain and evil queen conquered much of the world and ruled it from within these walls." Her face was shrouded inside her black hood, but Arthur had the distinct impression Mrs. Dumphry didn't like telling this story.

"One day," she continued, "a poet arrived in the city. No one knew where the man had come from, but this poet spoke words of such beauty that all who heard them were transformed." Mrs. Dumphry stopped speaking as they passed a particularly large group of small, wobbling creatures. The things only came up to Arthur's knees and reminded him of both lizard and bird.

"The poet spoke of a new way to live," Mrs. Dumphry said after they'd passed the creatures. "He spoke of freedom and joy and beauty and laughter. But the queen had never known true freedom, and she mistrusted the poet. When the queen's most trusted adviser told her to kill the poet, she did."

Arthur felt cold as he listened to Mrs. Dumphry's words. "As the poet died, the queen's adviser revealed his true identity. He was not a human at all, but a usurper from another world—the Assassin. And in the moment of the poet's death, the Shadowfog was born."

She sighed. "Within minutes, the Shadowfog had covered every inch of the city. And every living human and beast had been transformed into monsters and shadows. Many of the creatures and shadows you see now were once the inhabitants of this city."

Arthur felt a shiver run down his spine. "So what happened to the queen?" he asked. "Did she also become a monster?"

Mrs. Dumphry turned and looked Arthur in the eyes. Her cheeks were wet with tears. "No," she said as a small smile formed at the corners of her lips. "The queen did not become a monster. As the poet lay dying, she begged his forgiveness. And he forgave her. He spoke words of such beauty that they transformed her soul. Then her eyes began to burn, and the once-evil queen became the first member of the Awakened."

Arthur lowered his eyes as a creature that was part bear and part octopus slumped past.

"The Assassin demanded the queen bow before him," Mrs. Dumphry continued. "He threatened to kill her if she did not. And the queen had no doubt he would do it. She was trapped and could think of no escape." Mrs. Dumphry stopped for a moment as a look of wonder filled her eyes. "And just as the Assassin was about to take her life, she heard it."

"Heard what?"

"The voice of the poet."

Five thousand, twenty-four years, and two days earlier

Jack huddled behind the pillar, cradling Time in his arms. She was pale and barely breathing. He stroked her hair and peeked out again.

"I will not serve you!" the queen cried. She squinted at the Assassin as if her eyes were suddenly sensitive to the light. "I've been blinded my whole life. But my eyes have been opened. And I will not bow!"

"You have chosen poorly," the Assassin rasped. Black lightning exploded from his fingers but stopped just before it touched the queen, sizzling and snapping and straining. The Assassin stepped closer, but still the lightning did not touch her.

The queen looked as shocked as he did.

"The scales!" the Assassin screamed. "What have you done? Where are your scales?" He peered into the queen's eyes as his own flamed brightly.

"Did you truly think death could hold me?" a voice said.

Jack gasped. The poet was alive and standing! And he was also somehow … more. His eyes gathered light, and as he stepped forward, the wound in his side stitched itself into a scar.

"I killed you!" the Assassin screamed. "You cannot come back! It was agreed! If I could steal their hearts, if I could turn them against you, this world would be mine!"

"It was agreed." The poet nodded. "But I will not abandon my children. If there is but one who believes in me, I will not leave her to you." The poet looked at the queen, then turned his attention back to the Assassin. "The Last Battle is nearly upon us, and the end of this story will be told. The child will be born without scales, and the final choice will be made."

The Assassin threw his head back and howled. The throne room trembled as pillars collapsed and debris began to fall. Jack dragged Time away and scrambled to hide behind a small pile of rubble. When he looked again, the poet and the queen were gone.

The Assassin's voice quavered with rage. "I will enslave your children, and they will worship me for it. I will plunge this world into never-ending darkness, and they will sing my praises. Alive or dead, your children will reject you and they will call me Father!"

After a moment he continued. "The child will serve me. The child will love me. And the child will destroy your children." Then he stormed from the chamber.

As Jack sat in stunned silence, a figure in a dark cloak scurried out from behind a pillar and approached the throne. It studied the ground where the poet's body had been, then darted after the Assassin.

With the Assassin gone and the throne room empty, Time stood and watched Jack with wide eyes. "That's my favorite part so far," she said. "Out of everything, that's my favorite!"

"I don't understand," Jack said. "That was terrible!"

"Oh, it was the worst thing ever." Time nodded. "But I'm talking about the end part, when the poet rose from the dead and saved Mrs. Dumphry ... that's my favorite! Did you like it?"

"I suppose so, yes," Jack said after some thought. "But I don't understand! How is the poet still alive? I saw him die."

"Yes. That was terrible," Time agreed. "But why must you keep talking about that part? The next part is the best. It makes me happy every time I think about it!"

"But I don't understand!"

Time giggled. "I don't either, silly! But what does that matter? Now, are you going to get the pen or what?"

Jack blinked. He'd forgotten all about the pen. "Why do I need to—" *Could it be?* He walked to the place where the poet had died, and he picked up the pen from the bloodied floor. He pulled the ancient pen from his jacket pocket and compared the two. There was no question: the quill King Edward had given him was the same quill, only five thousand years later.

"What is it for?" he asked.

"Well, I suppose it's for writing!" Time snickered.

"Right," Jack said slowly, "but why do I need it?"

"I don't know! But I'm sure you do."

Jack was about to ask what he was supposed to do with it when she grabbed his hand. And suddenly Jack heard his note. He heard the ring of time, and he knew what to do. He closed his eyes and embraced its call. In less than a heartbeat, Jack and Time were flying backward through the air.

"I've always wished I could fly," Time said when they landed. "Did you know Elion can fly? All Sephari can. But that's the closest I ever get. It's fun, though, right?"

It was hard not to be in a good mood with Time. She was full of wonder and quick to laugh. Jack smiled. "Yes, it is."

They were standing in the middle of a group of stone huts and caves. The forest was thick all around them, and it was very quiet.

"Where are we?" he asked. Then he added, "When are we?"

"Oh, it's just a few years later. But don't worry, we're on the other side of the world and far away from the evil city."

"What are we doing here?" he asked.

"P-please, don't hurt me!"

Jack spun to see a young boy, flat on his back, staring wide-eyed. He reminded Jack of someone, though he couldn't imagine whom.

"We're not going to hurt you," Jack said. He offered a hand and pulled the boy up.

"How did you do it?" the boy breathed. "You just appeared out of nowhere! Are you ... magicians?"

Time snickered. "Magicians! That's so funny!"

"No, we are not magicians," Jack said with a smile. "We are just here to—" He stopped and turned to Time. "Why are we here?"

"You must be ... are you ... are you members of the Awakened?" the boy asked cautiously.

With those words, Jack knew who the boy reminded him of. Standing in front of him was a five-thousand-year-old ancestor of King Edward. "Yes," Jack said. "Yes, I am one of the Awakened. And

I have an important mission for you." He fished the new pen from his pocket.

Present day

Arthur watched as Mrs. Dumphry, Aias, and Andreal were dragged away by the savage mob. He couldn't believe it. Mrs. Dumphry had been about to tell Arthur about the poet when a Shadule slithered by and recognized her. The creature's shriek had drawn every dark servant within twenty blocks.

Arthur was alone in the City of Shadows.

Andreal hadn't wasted a second. The moment they were spotted, he'd ripped off Arthur's black-and-silver cloak; underneath Arthur still wore Jack's Atherial Cloak. "It be up to you now, Lightning Dancer," Andreal said in the confusion. "Get the girl and get out; do no' be trying to save us!"

Before Andreal could say another word, the Shadow Souled swarmed over them while Arthur scrambled away.

Mrs. Dumphry and the others hadn't tried to fight. They were impossibly outnumbered and knew there was no chance of escape. Arthur watched as his friends were beaten senseless within seconds.

He tried to slow his breathing. *How I can rescue Alexia by myself?* Arthur stood with his back against the wall for more than three hours, far too terrified to move. He searched his mind but could think of nothing. Even if he could find Alexia, how was he supposed to help her escape a city of monsters?

But he couldn't stay on the street forever. Night was coming and the last thing he wanted was to be alone in the City of Shadows past dark.

Mrs. Dumphry had been leading them toward a palace in the center of the city, and Arthur decided it was as good a place as any. It must have hundreds of rooms—thousands maybe. With the Atherial Cloak to hide him, maybe he could find an empty room where he could spend the night.

Chapter 21

A DECISION MADE

Alexia was on her way back to the coliseum. When she had told Belial she would accept her role as High Princess of Thaltorose, he had been so happy that he'd demanded that all citizens make their way to the arena so they could hear the announcement.

Each step darkened her mood. As the choking coldness grew, Alexia came to terms with her decision. She'd accepted Belial's offer and together they would rule the world. She just needed to make herself hard enough so her heart wouldn't be hurt again. She needed to grow up and stop dreaming. Her father might not be a good man, but he was still her father.

She glanced up at him as he walked beside her. *I will make you proud*, she thought, *no matter what I have to do!*

Belial walked with them. *It's strange*, she thought; *he doesn't smell bad anymore*. The aroma wafting from the wound in his belly had a sweet smell to it; the sweat that dripped from his face and hands made his diamond skin shine all the brighter. Belial was more powerful than anyone. *And I will rule alongside him.*

More than one hundred thousand of Belial's servants had gathered in the coliseum. Every citizen of Thaltorose was there. And as Belial, Korah, and Alexia entered, the multitude stood and cheered wildly. Alexia gasped at the enormity of the arena and the vast numbers of creatures and humans in the stands. The crowd thundered as she waved to them. *These are my people*, she thought. *This is my army!*

Alexia followed Belial and her father to the far side of the arena, where two monstrous thrones of gold had been placed on a dais. A few paces in front of the thrones a fire burned brightly. Belial sat on the larger of the two thrones and motioned for Alexia to sit beside him. Her throne was smaller and a few paces back, but it was still impressive.

Alexia turned to her father, who nodded his approval. She nodded back, and as she sat, the crowd shrieked in delight. Korah stepped onto the dais and stood stiffly at Alexia's right hand.

After a moment, a strange creature Alexia hadn't noticed stepped onto the dais. Its body was sleek and silvery, and it had mirrors for eyes. As the creature raised its arms, the multitude quieted.

"It is with great pleasure," it said, "that I present the Child of Prophecy, the noble lady who will lead our army, the High Princess of Thaltorose!" The arena vibrated with the screams of the feverish crowd.

Five thousand, eleven years, and two days earlier

Jack and Time had been walking for more than an hour, but he was still thinking about his encounter with King Edward's young ancestor. "What I can't figure out is why I had to give the pen away. Why couldn't I have kept it? I had it in my hands. It seems silly to give it away so I can get it back again in thousands of years."

"You would never have known it was important if you hadn't got it from the king first!" Time said.

"Yes, but … that really doesn't make sense," Jack said. He tried not to think about it.

"Why must everything always make sense?" Time asked. "It's the mysterious things that are most fun!"

Jack just shook his head and smiled. "Where do we go from here?" he asked.

"There is someone you need to meet," Time said. "You're going to like him very much. Time stopped in front of a small cottage and grabbed Jack's hands. "I need to leave now, Jack Staples. I've shown you everything you need to see."

"What? You can't leave. I don't even know when or where I am. How am I supposed to get back? And what am I meant to do? And what about Alexia? Don't we need to help her?"

"You ask a lot of questions!" Time giggled. "But I think most questions aren't really about answers. I think most questions are about confidence. And you should always be confident—because you know your note! Remember, you can plan things, but in the end it's always better to let your note direct you."

"But—"

Time wrapped him in a fierce hug. "I believe in you, Jack Staples."

And then, just like that, she flew backward out of his arms and high into the sky, giggling the whole way.

Jack let out a long breath. He was alone in a strange land, in another time without a clue of what to do or how to get back.

"Hello, Jack."

Jack jumped, and found himself standing before a man in a patchwork cloak.

Arthur Greaves sprinted up fifty flights of stairs without stopping for a breather.

When he had first entered the palace, he'd been excited to find it completely empty. Except for those shadows at the corners of his vision, he hadn't seen or heard a single creature. Wherever the inhabitants of this city had gone, it seemed all of them had gone together. But before he'd gone more than a few steps, a dark, slithering fog appeared behind him.

Arthur was certain it was the Shadowfog Jack had told him about. The slithering darkness didn't seem to be able to see him, but Arthur thought it might be able to smell him, because it followed slowly, as if uncertain he was there. When Arthur found himself in the stairwell, he began to climb. But the fog followed him up.

After fifty flights, he could barely breathe. If the fog was still following, it was somewhere far below. He stumbled down a wide hall and pushed through two golden doors. And gasped.

I must be in the throne room! The chamber was so large he couldn't see where it ended. In its center was a mammoth throne made of gold and gemstones; off to the side was an enormous statue. Fires burned throughout the chamber and torches lined the walls, but the shadows surrounding the flames were darker than they should have been. Each pool of light fought hard to shine in this place.

Arthur walked toward the throne, shivering. This chamber felt even more wrong than the city, as if it were the source of the stench that permeated everything. Yet he couldn't leave. Something was drawing him forward, pulling him toward the throne.

The throne was solid gold and as large as the blacksmith shop back in Ballylesson. Golden stairs climbed to a gigantic seat, and Arthur took the first step. He didn't want to, but he felt like he needed to. Whatever was drawing him forward was at the top. And as he arrived, he spotted it.

A small, carved wooden box floated before the seat. It spun slowly, surrounded by a pulsating darkness. As he looked at it, Arthur had the distinct impression the box was trying to escape the darkness. When he moved, it shifted toward him, vibrating and pressing against the shadows.

As if by magic, words appeared on the side of the box. Arthur had to squint to read them through the shadows. "ARTHUR GREAVES: LOYAL. COURAGEOUS. WARRIOR."

Feeling as if he were in a dream, Arthur reached for the box, but the moment his fingers touched the darkness, they burned like fire. He whipped his hand back and watched throbbing blisters form on his fingers. He looked again at the box and knew he couldn't give up. He didn't think he was courageous or a warrior of any kind, though he did try his best to be loyal. He had no idea what the box was, but he would not leave without it. He hated the idea of anything being trapped in this place.

Jack gaped at the poet.

"Won't you come in and join me for tea?" The poet's smile was warm and inviting. He stood on the stoop of a very ordinary-looking cottage.

"Yes. Yes, sir, I mean. Your Majesty or ..." Jack could feel his face turn red. "I would love to."

"I've been looking forward to seeing you again!" The poet smiled and stepped inside. A teapot and two cups were laid out on the table. "Please sit down."

"Thank you," Jack said numbly. "But I ... I think you may be mistaken. We've never met."

"Oh, sure we have, lots of times!" The poet winked as he poured the tea. The smell of fresh mint made Jack smile. It was the same kind of tea his mother used to make.

"When did we meet? I'm not saying you're wrong, only that I'm sure I would have remembered."

"Not only have you met me"—the poet's eyes sparkled like his smile—"but you have been me."

Jack stopped the cup before it touched his lips. *Is it possible that with all that's happened the poet has somehow … lost his marbles?*

The poet burst out laughing. "I assure you, all of my marbles are intact!" He wiped a tear from his eye. "But you are very funny. It's one of the many things I love about you."

Jack's jaw dropped. The poet had just read his thoughts. He should be embarrassed, but somehow he didn't mind.

"What do you mean, I've been you?" Jack asked.

"You were me the day you tried to rescue Arthur from the bully in the schoolyard." The poet sipped his tea. "You've been me more times than I could possibly mention over a single cup of tea. Whenever you choose to love others, you are my hands and my breath." As the poet leaned forward, Jack leaned in as well. He wanted to be as close to him as possible.

"You see, Jack, when you were born, a part of my spirit was woven into yours, and my blood flows in your veins. It is the same with all humans. And if you were to fully embrace who you are, nothing in this universe could stand against you."

Jack wasn't sure he understood a word the poet was saying, but he wanted to hear more.

"Your life does not end when you die; this world is just the beginning of the most fantastical adventure you could imagine."

The bells were ringing. Jack's note sounded in his chest. The poet heard them too.

"I'm afraid the tea is finished," he said. "Your sister needs your help, Jack. She's about to face an impossible choice, and she will need you soon."

Jack didn't want to leave. He stood, then hesitated. "May I ask you something?"

"Of course," the poet said.

"Are we going to win? Are we going to defeat the Assassin?"

"Ah, now that is the question. But what fun is a story if you already know the ending? I will tell you this: the Assassin has only the power you give him. He can win this war. If you give him the power, he will take it. But I believe in you, and I am always with you."

The poet touched his shoulder, and Jack exploded backward through the door and high into the air. As he watched the small house shrink into the distance, Jack began to laugh. He had no idea where he was going, but he didn't care. He trusted the poet.

In the circus, Alexia had grown accustomed to large crowds cheering her on, but it had been nothing like this. The circus tent held five hundred people. The arena of Thaltorose held over a hundred thousand beasts, creatures, and humans—and it was filled to bursting!

This is what I was made for, she thought. Alexia had forgotten what it felt like to have crowds cheering her every move. Without thinking, she sprang from her throne and vaulted over the fire, twisting her body into a spinning double flip. As she landed, the crowd shrieked its delight. Alexia rolled into a handspring and spun, kicking her legs out like a spinning top. She was about to leap into a front flip when she saw the furious look in her father's eyes.

She lost focus, stumbled, and fell flat. The crowd's roar turned to jeers. Her cheeks grew hot as she took a deep breath and walked stiffly back to her throne.

"What are you doing?" her father said. "I tell you to stop acting like a child and you do this? We never steal praise from the Shadow Lord, not ever!" Korah was shaking.

As she sat, Alexia stole a glance at Belial, and yes, there was the fire of jealousy in his eyes. It was gone in a flash, but Alexia shivered. She had been hoping to make Belial and her father proud. *How could Belial possibly be jealous of me?*

"The games are about to begin," her father said. "Do not shame me again!"

As Alexia's father stepped back from her throne, the silvery creature raised its arms, silencing the crowd. "Bring out the prisoners!" The catlike creature's purring voice echoed throughout the arena. Whispers of expectation rose.

What prisoners? Alexia felt a growing sense of dread.

A small door slid open at the opposite end of the coliseum. Three men and two women dressed in rags were shoved into the arena by a Shadule carrying a barbed spear. Heavy chains fastened wrists and legs, causing them to crouch low as they walked. As they neared the center of the arena, a low-throated growl rose from the crowd.

"What's happening?" Alexia asked.

Her father smiled coldly and nodded at the approaching prisoners. "Watch," he said.

The silvery creature quieted the assembly. "You stand accused of joining the rebel group who calls themselves 'Awakened'," the creature rasped. Hisses and growls erupted from the crowd. "Yet the Shadow Lord is sympathetic to your plight. Today, in honor of the new High Princess of Thaltorose, he offers you ... mercy."

Astonished gasps rippled through the watching horde.

"Reject your allegiance to the rebels and bow to your new gods." The creature motioned toward Belial and Alexia. "Vow to fight for the Lord of Shadows and the Princess of Thaltorose," the creature hissed. "Vow to kill for them, and in their great mercy they will forgive your betrayal!"

A hushed silence spread through the mass of man, beast, and creature as they waited to see what would happen. Alexia wanted to scream. She didn't need these people to bow to her! *But if it will save their lives, surely they will do it!*

One of the men shuffled forward, and when he looked at Belial, there was only pity in his eyes. "We follow the Author, the maker of story and creator of all things. And though you may take our lives, we will not bow before you, Assassin!"

The man looked at Alexia. "My lady, we have awaited your arrival since the beginning. I heard of your valor in the battle of Agartha. I do not know what this monster has told you, but he is a deceiver. He is the father of lies and—"

The man clutched his chest. Belial stood with his arm outstretched as the man dropped to his knees and gasped for breath. His skin turned a stony gray and began to crack. When the man's arms shattered, he grimaced. As the rest of his body turned to stone, he let out a final gasp and crashed to the ground.

The crowd hooted and howled. Alexia stood with arms out-stretched, struggling to breathe. Belial had murdered the man for no reason.

Alexia's father was by her side. "Sit down!" he said. "This is your life now. This is what you have chosen. There can be no mercy in the Shadow Army."

Tears welled in her eyes, but she blinked them away. She would not be a child! She would not let her father see her cry. She would do what had to be done!

Belial's eyes shone with a rapturous glow as he sat back down. The silvery creature quieted the crowd and fixed its attention on the remaining prisoners. "You are out of time," it said grandly. "Will you bow before the Lord of Shadows?"

One by one the prisoners knelt, all but one woman who stood defiantly with fists clenched. As she looked at those kneeling beside her, she shook her head sadly. "Choosing to follow this monster is a fate far worse than death. Do not replace sight with blindness! Do not lose heart!"

Those kneeling didn't meet the woman's eyes. One by one they said the words. They rejected the Awakened and vowed to serve the Assassin and the High Princess of Thaltorose. Alexia watched, feeling both relief and sadness. *They did the right thing*, she thought. *They saved their lives!*

The woman who was standing watched as her friends were led away. Desperation rose inside Alexia. *Why won't you just kneel? You must bow!* She could stand it no longer. "Please, my lady!" As Belial stood, she leaped up beside him. "You must kneel! You must! It will save your life!"

"You are the Child of Prophecy," the woman said. "And you are good. This"—she glanced around the arena—"is not who you are. You must not allow your light to die, my girl. And you must not fear for me. Death is not the end; it is merely a new beginning." She smiled at Alexia just before she fell backward and shattered on the arena floor.

The crowd let out a guttural roar, and Belial basked in their praise. Alexia sat down hard. She struggled to see through the tears in her eyes. The woman's smile … it was the first real smile she'd received since coming to Thaltorose.

The silvery creature threw its arms wide and screamed, "And now for the main event!"

A large trapdoor in the arena floor slid open, and a platform began to rise. Hulking in the center of the platform was a Drogule holding a cable of electrified light. The cable sizzled and snapped, splitting into nine different directions to loop around nine captives. The cable wrapped their bodies, holding them stiffly in place.

The platform held all five members of her Gang of Rogues.

"No!" Alexia whispered. *No.*

Standing stiffly beside her friends from Belfast stood a giant and three others—Wild, Aias, and Mrs. Dumphry. All watched Alexia with haunted eyes.

The eruption from the crowd was so frenzied Alexia wanted to tear at her ears. She wanted to hide; she hated the idea of Wild or the others seeing her sitting beside Belial, dressed in his colors. But she could feel her father's eyes on her back. She had made her decision, hadn't she?

Alexia wanted to scream at Mrs. Dumphry. All of this was her fault! She was the one who killed the poet! She was the one who dragged Alexia and Jack, Arthur, and even Wild into this whole mess. She was the reason Alexia was in this impossible situation!

"Before the sun sets," the silvery creature said to the audience, "in honor of the new High Princess, these rebels will be put to death!" The crowd thundered its bloodthirsty glee. Then the creature turned to Alexia. "The end is near. The choice must be made. The child must bow!"

As the crowd roared, Alexia's father knelt and presented her cloak and sling. Alexia gaped when she saw them.

"You must reject the Awakened and bow before Belial," her father said, handing her the cloak and sling. "You must vow to serve him always, and you must throw these in the fire as a sign that you have fully rejected your old life. And you must do these things now. Only when it is done will you truly be the High Princess of Thaltorose!"

Alexia felt hot tears running down her cheeks. She looked at the cloak and sling, then back at the prisoners.

"You must do this, Daughter. This is what you were born for … It is what your mother and I always wanted for you!"

Alexia couldn't stop crying. The last flicker of warmth faded inside her. "What did you used to call me, Father?" Her voice trembled.

"What?"

"You had a nickname for me when I was little. I used to sit on your lap and pull on your beard and you held me close and called me something. What was it?"

"This is not the time," he said. "Everyone is waiting. We can talk of this later!"

"Tell me!" Alexia cried. "What did you call me?"

"It was a very long time ago. What does it matter now?" Her father grabbed her shoulders roughly and stood her up. "You have been nothing but a disappointment to me. Now do as I command!" Rage shone in his eyes.

"Yes, Father." Alexia bit her lip, feeling the block of ice grow inside her chest. *You can do this!* she told herself. *Stop acting like a child and bow!*

Except for the expectant whispers from the crowd, relative quiet had fallen. Belial smiled in anticipation, and this time the smile did reach his eyes.

As she stepped forward, Alexia felt something hard and cold between her fingers. She hadn't realized she'd placed her hand in her cloak pocket. *It's Father's Memory Stone!* She'd forgotten all about the small blue-veined stone she'd taken from his bedchamber. As she stepped toward Belial, she closed her hand around it and whispered, "Show me the memory of my parents."

Belial gave Alexia a curious look. And as Alexia took another step toward the throne, the world shifted.

Chapter 22

THE CHILD BOWS

When Alexia opened her eyes, she was no longer in the arena. The Memory Stone had taken her to the kitchen of the house she'd grown up in. Her breath caught when she saw her mother standing at the kitchen table, spreading frosting on a strawberry cake. Her father stood behind, wrapping her in a loving embrace.

Tears sprang to Alexia's eyes. They were not tears of sadness but joy. These were her parents. These were the people she belonged to. The man who held her mother may have looked like Korah, but it was not him; she was sure of it. This man was loving and kind, and Alexia could never imagine him screaming at her.

Alexia began looking around the kitchen. If this was Korah's memory, surely he must be here somewhere. *There!* She spotted him. He was standing outside the kitchen window staring in.

The kitchen door shattered, a Shadule standing in the entry.

Her father grabbed a knife from the kitchen counter. "Go!" he yelled. "I'll find you both as soon as I can."

Alexia screamed as the Shadule struck. Her mother ran from the room as her father wrestled the creature to the ground.

Alexia blinked. Now she was standing outside the house by the front door. *Korah must have left the window.* She could still hear the sounds of the battle coming from the kitchen, but Korah wasn't interested in her father. He snarled as he slammed his boot into the front door, splintering it off the hinges to reveal Alexia's mother darting down the stairs.

"You!" she cried.

Black fire shot from Korah's hands to explode against her mother's chest.

"No!" Alexia shrieked as Korah grabbed her mother roughly, pulling her to her feet.

A bloodcurdling scream sounded from the kitchen, and her father stormed through the door and spotted Korah holding his wife hostage.

"You!" he raged. "You are behind this?"

"Hello, Brother," Korah snarled. His pale blade was pressed hard against her mother's neck.

"You dare come here? You bring the Shadow Souled into my house?"

Alexia watched numbly. She knew what would happen. This was only a memory and she could not change it.

"The great darkness is coming and there is nothing you can do to stop it. Yet you will not live to see the Last Battle." Korah smiled coldly. "Your time has come, Brother!"

"You came here to … to kill me?" Her father seemed confused.

"Don't act so surprised. You must have known this day would come." Korah pressed the blade deeper into Madeleine Dreager's neck as a slow trickle of blood dripped down. "I've been hunting the Awakened for years now, killing you off one by one. But I will enjoy this day more than most."

"Where does your hatred come from?" Her father shook his head sadly. "Did I wrong you without knowing? Did I do something so unforgiveable?"

"I have hated you since the day we were born." Korah seethed. "I've dreamed of this day for longer than you could imagine."

Alexia's mother met her father's eyes and gave an almost imperceptible glance toward the window.

Her father's eyes flicked over and back again so quickly Alexia wondered if she'd imagined it. The tiniest smile spread his lips. There was a child stalking through the woods. The much younger Alexia wore her brand-new red dress and was creeping into the forest, stopping every few steps to examine a stone.

Alexia remembered the moment. She'd been searching for the perfect stones to use in her new sling.

"How could we be so different, you and I?" Her father took one step forward. "The only thing you have ever loved was power. You sat on the Council of Seven, and still it wasn't enough. But when you turned your back on us, I never dreamed you would join the Shadow Souled."

"The Council of Seven!" Korah scoffed. "Fools, all of them. And I was a fool to want to be one of them. I—" Korah's eyes landed on Alexia's coat lying crumpled on the floor. A cold smile crept onto his lips. "Tell me, Brother, do I have a niece or a nephew?"

Korah didn't know I existed!

"You can threaten me," her father said coldly, "but if you speak of my child again, I will end you."

Alexia almost stepped back from the dangerous look in her father's eyes.

"You haven't changed a bit. You are not in command here; I am!" Korah snarled.

Korah barked a command at the wounded Shadule. "Find the child and bring it to me."

The Shadule hissed excitedly and darted up the stairs. Alexia watched her younger self disappear into the woods.

"I love you, Madeleine Dreager," her father said sadly. "Look after our little goat."

Her mother nodded as a thin sliver of light flashed between them. In the blink of an eye, her mother had disappeared and her father stood in her place.

Korah screamed when he found himself holding the sword against his brother's neck. Alexia's father used the confusion to slam the back of his head into Korah's face. Korah stumbled back as blood burst from his nose. Yet even as her father turned to fight, Korah pierced him with the blade.

"No," her father groaned as he dropped to the floor.

"No!" Alexia gasped in unison.

Just then the Shadule arrived at the bottom of the stairs. "There is no child here," the creature rasped.

Korah grimaced as he looked at his dying brother. "I promise you this, I will find Madeleine, and I will find your child. And I will kill them."

"You have always been blind." Her father groaned. "And you will lose this war." As his eyes began to glaze over, he turned and looked directly at Alexia. "I love you, my little goat." Thick blood dripped from his chin. "I love you with all my heart."

Alexia gasped. She didn't know if he was truly looking at her or was merely seeing things as he died, but his words were like life to her soul.

"Pathetic." Korah grimaced. As he stalked from the house, he kicked over a lampstand; oil and fire exploded along the wall.

"Make sure he's dead," Korah commanded the Shadule.

Alexia heard the creature's excited hiss as the world shifted once again.

Alexia blinked. Although minutes had passed in the memory, no time at all seemed to have passed in the real world. She took the final step toward the Assassin's throne and stopped. She was standing before him with her head bowed. Alexia hesitated only a moment before dropping to her knees at the feet of the Assassin. The mob howled.

She didn't feel like crying, and she didn't want to scream at Korah for deceiving her. She didn't even want to yell at the Assassin. She'd bowed so they wouldn't see her smile. After a moment, quiet fell once again as the assembly eagerly awaited what would come next. As she knelt before the creature Belial, warmth exploded in Alexia's chest. She was happier now than she'd been in ages. *Korah is not my father*, she thought. *The Assassin is pure evil.*

Alexia didn't understand what had happened with the poet and what she'd seen in the Assassin's memory, but none of that mattered. Right now all she wanted to do was laugh.

My father was a good man! The thought broadened her smile. And if she understood what she'd seen, there was a chance her mother was still alive!

"Child!" Korah knelt by her side. "Why are you waiting? You must say the words! Do you hear me? You must swear fealty to your new master!"

The stench from the wound in the Assassin's belly made Alexia want to retch, but she forced the feeling down. Instead, she turned to Korah and smiled as she dropped the Memory Stone onto the marble dais. Korah seemed confused by it; but after a moment his eyes widened.

"Alley Goat," Alexia said quietly as she looked down at her red cloak and sling. "My father called me Alley Goat." She couldn't help but laugh as a look of horror crossed Korah's face.

"My name is Alexia Dreager," she said in a loud voice. "And I am one of the two Children of Prophecy." The horde of humans, monsters, and beasts roared their approval. When Alexia met the Assassin's eyes, she offered a knowing smile. "I came here today to swear allegiance to your master."

The Assassin watched her with uncertain eyes. He'd seen the Memory Stone and the look on Korah's face.

Alexia stood and began to laugh. The sound was so foreign that the throngs of Shadow Souled went abruptly silent. Her laughter pierced the arena like a ray of sunshine in an underground cavern.

"But I know now that this creature sitting before me is not worthy of my allegiance or yours." When Alexia pointed at the Assassin, she raised her voice ever louder. "He is a liar and a murderer. He is the Assassin, and though it may be hard, we must stand against him. We must resist! Join me!" she shouted. "Join the Awakened!"

Silence engulfed the arena. Alexia turned to look at her friends, who still stood stiffly bound by the cables of electrified light. Wild raised his eyebrows as if to say, "Nice speech. Now what?"

Alexia turned to face the Assassin and took an involuntary step back. Darkness radiated from him, and his eyes were fiery. He stood before his throne with the Shadowfog boiling at his feet. It was a terrifying sight.

"Forget the games," the Assassin screamed as he raised his arms to the gathered mob. "The Last Battle begins now! Kill them all!"

The tens of thousands of Shadow Souled suddenly became an army of darkness as beast, monster, and human swarmed the arena. In the sky above, the winged creatures plummeted downward in an attempt to be the first to tear the Awakened to pieces.

Alexia didn't waste a second. Even as Korah drew his sword, she leaped from the dais and sprinted toward the Drogule holding the cord of electrified light. At best she'd have a few seconds to defeat the Drogule and free her friends. There was no chance of escape. That had never been a possibility. But if she didn't free them from the

Drogule, every one of her friends would be torn to shreds without even having a chance to fight back.

Even above the roar of the mob, the demonic laughter of the Assassin echoed.

Chapter 23

A MOUNTAIN
OF DARKNESS

Jack ran toward the mammoth coliseum. He'd been following the roars of a screaming crowd ever since he'd entered the City of Shadows. The gates had been left unguarded, and every street was as still and quiet as the grave.

When he'd been with Time in the garden, he'd seen a vision of this place. He knew this is where he would find Alexia, Arthur, and the others. Even as he ran toward the sounds of bloodthirsty cries, there was peace inside him. Jack didn't know what he was meant to do, but he knew he was meant to be here, and that was enough. It wouldn't be possible to stop what was happening. He was just a boy. Yet this is where the poet had sent him.

He wasn't just the poet! Jack thought. *He was the Author!* His heart still pounded at the memory. And as he ran toward a fight he knew he could not win, Jack smiled.

Arthur wanted to cry as he stared at his burned hand. He'd tried multiple times to grab the small box from its dark prison. His fingers were blistered, and the smell of seared flesh made bile rise in the back of his throat.

He circled the box that hovered above the enormous throne. He wanted to leave it. But he could not. He felt foolish as he reread the words on it. "ARTHUR GREAVES: LOYAL. COURAGEOUS. WARRIOR." They seemed to mock him.

Arthur squeezed his eyes shut. *What am I doing here? I'm just a boy. I don't even know why I'm trying to get this stupid box!* He wiped a tear from his eye and remembered the last thing Elion had said to him. *"Arthur Greaves, you are powerful and courageous."* Her eyes had blazed with a golden light. They had been standing in the chamber below Buckingham Palace as the World Portal spun behind her. *"And something tells me that if this mission has any chance of success, it will be because you were there."*

Arthur straightened his back and stepped toward the box once again. "I am not here by accident," he whispered. "I am Arthur Greaves, and I am one of the Awakened." After a moment he smiled and added,

"And I am the Lightning Dancer." Without thinking, Arthur began to move his feet in a way he had never moved them before, though it felt perfectly natural. Before long, a tornado of electricity had formed around him, and where he moved, liquid light moved with him.

The electricity called to him, wrapping him in its embrace. Again he reached for the box, and this time the darkness imprisoning it shrieked and exploded away. And just like that, the box dropped and tumbled down the golden stairs.

Arthur stopped his dancing and began to laugh as he ran down the stairs and picked up the wooden box.

As Alexia ran toward her friends, the Drogule roared and yanked the cord of electrified light. All nine Awakened groaned as the cable tightened around them. They watched her helplessly.

Alexia took the last steps and hurled her body into the light that bound her friends. The moment she touched it, electricity blasted through her body, causing her to stiffen and jerk uncontrollably. Yet as the cable wrapped itself around her, it ceased to bind the Awakened.

Andreal dove at the Drogule, wrestling it to the ground and ripping the sizzling cable from its hands, freeing Alexia. She lay flat on her back, trying to catch her breath.

Wild stood with his arm outstretched. "There's no time to nap." He smiled. "Now is the time to fight." He pulled Alexia to her feet just in time to turn and face the swarm of tens of thousands of Shadow Souled.

Alexia wanted to talk to her friends, to apologize for not standing with them sooner, but she didn't even have time to meet their eyes. The horde of dark servants was upon them. A moment before the flood crashed into the Awakened from every direction, a shield of blue light sprang up around them. The shield was the only thing between the Awakened and a crushing death.

The dark servants howled as they slammed into the shield. From every side the Shadow Souled pressed against the wall of thin blue light. The snarling faces of monster, beast, and human were everywhere. The sky was no longer visible as winged creatures pummeled the shield from above.

"I can't hold it any longer!" Mrs. Dumphry shouted. Her shield buckled inward, splintering into a thousand pieces, and the mountain of dark servants was on them.

It wasn't fighting—there was no room to fight or to move at all. The dark servants were consumed with bloodlust. Both Awakened and dark servants began to scream as the pressure built, those in the center being crushed to death in a melee of bodies pushing in from behind and above.

Alexia couldn't find the breath to scream. There was too little room to draw breath. *This is it*, she thought. *This is where we die.* It was a cold thought. The pressure became unbearable, squeezing from every direction. She looked at the crazed beasts, humans, and monsters, gritted her teeth, then closed her eyes, trying to stay conscious through the pain.

Suddenly, a burst of wind exploded from somewhere nearby and ripped through the crush of bodies. And the immense pressure stopped growing. Alexia opened her eyes—at least five out of every seven dark servants looked as if they'd fallen unconscious. They hadn't dropped to the ground because there was no room for them to fall. Alexia still couldn't draw a breath, but at least the pressure wasn't growing.

"What just happened?" Josiah groaned.

"They're sleeping!" Juno gasped.

"It canna be possible!" Andreal rumbled from somewhere beneath the mountain of flesh. Alexia could hear him shoving against the bodies, yet even Andreal wasn't strong enough to shift the mammoth heap.

The dark servants who hadn't fallen unconscious still snarled and howled, but they, too, were trapped in the crush of bodies.

"What's that?" Wild said.

Alexia also heard it. A crackling and snapping sound, growing louder by the second. The air became electric; her skin pricked and her hair began to rise.

The mountain of dark servants was being shoved aside by a wall of liquid electricity, clearing a path to the small band of Awakened. Alexia dropped to her knees and gasped for breath. Spinning round in the clearing path was Arthur Greaves, electricity flowing from his outstretched hands.

He's dancing! Alexia realized.

When Arthur met Alexia's eyes, he blushed. "It seems to work better when I dance," he said sheepishly.

She stood and limped over to wrap him in a fierce hug. "I missed you!" Alexia said. "And your dancing is splendid. Truly it is!"

"I missed you too," Arthur said.

"Well done, Arthur," Mrs. Dumphry said as she strode toward them. "Well done, indeed! Before this war is over, you may be one of the most powerful Awakened to ever walk the earth!"

Arthur turned a deep shade of red. The look on his face was a mixture of pride and embarrassment.

"We have no time to waste," Mrs. Dumphry said. "The enemy is already stirring. We must be out of the arena before they awaken."

"It's only the animals that are unconscious," Josiah said, looking around.

Alexia stared dizzily at the mountain of Shadow Souled. Josiah was right—anything that looked even remotely like an animal was unconscious. The humanlike dark servants were still conscious but trapped beneath bodies or behind the wall of liquid light. That wouldn't last long.

She had a memory of standing in the ruined central market of Belfast. "I think I did this," she said. "Though I have no idea how."

"Let's not worry about it now," Mrs. Dumphry said. "We are running out of time. Arthur, you mustn't—"

Arthur dropped his hands, gasped, then fainted as the wall of fluid light evaporated, and the mountain of dark servants crumpled.

Mrs. Dumphry sighed. "You mustn't let go of your Soulprint too quickly," she said. "I feared this might happen. Young Mr. Greaves has exhausted himself beyond what is safe. Andreal, would you mind?"

Andreal threw Arthur over his shoulder as Mrs. Dumphry turned and sent streams of fire into a few dark servants who'd wriggled free from the crush. As the Awakened ran toward the arena exit, Alexia donned her cloak and inserted a stone into her sling. It felt so good to have them back.

"They're waking up," Aias warned.

"We need to free the others!" Juno called as they entered a darkened passageway. "There are at least five thousand Awakened in the dungeons below."

All eyes turned to Mrs. Dumphry. The old woman glanced into the arena as she assessed the situation. Thousands of the Shadow Souled were now awake, though most still wore a dazed look.

"What do you say, Alexia Dreager? The prophecy says you and young Jack Staples will lead the armies of the Awakened into the Last Battle. If it has truly started, then it is time for you to begin taking this responsibility. Shall we mount a rescue and face impossible odds, or shall we flee and live to fight another day?"

Alexia didn't want this responsibility. Yet when she met Josiah's eyes, she knew what they had to do. "We can't leave them behind," she said quickly. "We must try to free them at least!"

Mrs. Dumphry smiled. "You are showing the signs of a true leader, child. I told you once that the line between foolishness and courage is razor thin. In this case I do not know where it lies. Aias, Andreal, Wild, and I will hold this corridor for as long as we can. The rest of you go and free our people!"

Alexia turned to her old gang. "I let you down; I know that. And I was wrong. Will you forgive me? And will you follow me into the dungeons?"

"No," Josiah said. "I will not follow you because you have no idea where you're going." He broke into a wide grin as Juno chortled. "But I will forgive you. Now, follow us!"

Alexia turned and followed her gang into the dungeons.

Chapter 24

A TIMELY BATTLE

Jack Staples sprinted down an empty street in the City of Shadows. He was desperate to get to the coliseum to help his friends. The bloodthirsty cries resounding through the streets sent a chill down his spine.

At last it was in sight, and as he ran down the street leading to the arena, two bodies soared across the sky and crashed to the ground just in front of him. Jack stopped—it was the Assassin lying flat on his back with Jack Staples lying atop him. The Assassin was choking the other Jack.

"Nice trick, boy, but your Soulprint will not save you this time!" the Assassin snarled.

You're not going mad, Jack thought. *You have seen this before. It's just you from the future!*

The future Jack was dressed the same and turning an ashen gray. The Assassin stood, holding the other Jack by the neck, lifting him a pace above the ground. The other Jack met Jack's eyes.

Jack jumped as he realized he should probably be helping himself. He darted forward, unsheathing Ashandar and swinging the black blade wildly. But the Assassin spotted him; he leaped away and dropped the other Jack.

"Thanks." The other Jack fell to his knees, gasping for breath and rubbing his neck.

"No worries," Jack replied.

"Shall we end this?" the future Jack said grimly.

Jack took a deep breath and tried to sound fierce. "I'm ready if you are," he said. Ashandar warmed in his hands.

The Assassin sent black lightning at Jack, but he raised Ashandar high and the bolts dissipated as they struck the sword. The future Jack attacked from the opposite side, and Jack continued his own assault, moving only as he felt the sword prompting.

A blade of white fire appeared in the Assassin's hands. As he struck, Jack rolled away. When the Assassin's blade met the future Jack's sword, the air cracked and rippled as light and darkness exploded from them.

The Assassin began to rise from the burning street as the future Jack screamed and leaped onto his back, still holding Ashandar in his hands. Together, the Jack from the future and the Assassin soared away, disappearing into the clouds.

Jack sheathed Ashandar. *What just happened?* His chest tightened as the sound of one hundred thousand triumphant voices resounded through the streets and thousands of winged monsters fell from the sky toward the center of the mammoth coliseum.

Jack watched the falling monsters with a sense of dread. He ran toward the entrance once again, and skidded to a stop.

Striding out of the coliseum was the Assassin. His skin shimmered in the unearthly light, and his eyes were raging fire. He stopped when he saw Jack, a look of confusion sweeping his sweaty face.

Jack pulled back the hood of his cloak as he raised Ashandar high. "I am the Child of Prophecy," he said, "and I will not run away any longer." This was his destiny; this is what he was born to do.

"You!" The Assassin offered a grotesque smile. "You dare come here? To my city!" He threw his head back and howled with laughter. "You have arrived just in time. I've just killed the girl, and you are the last thing standing in my way."

Jack's heart sank. He was too late. That had to be what he'd heard inside the arena. *Alexia must be dead. Why else would the Assassin leave unless he was sure she was gone?*

"No!" Jack shouted. "I don't believe you. You are the deceiver. Alexia Dreager is still alive!" Another roar from the coliseum cut off to silence. The Assassin glanced back the way he'd come.

"You're worried," Jack said, "because you know I'm right. You will not win. I have met the Author! I know that he still lives. And the army of the Awakened will defeat you soon enough, Assassin!"

"You are wrong, child. This world belongs to me. And I have no more use for you in my world." Streams of liquid darkness exploded from the Assassin, while behind him, another Jack appeared, staring at Jack. In that moment Jack heard the ring of time and understood what he was meant to do. He embraced his note and flew backward through the air.

Jack landed behind the Assassin and met the eyes of the Jack from a few seconds earlier. As the black lightning passed through empty space, Jack saw himself fly backward and disappear. He didn't hesitate to strike with Ashandar, but the Assassin rose into the air, hovering just out of reach of Jack's blade.

The Assassin screamed as liquid darkness and molten lava shot from his hands to explode into the earth and buildings below. A split second before they struck, Jack sheathed Ashandar and embraced the bells. He looked up to see himself appear in the sky just above the Assassin.

Jack flew through time and appeared a split second earlier, high up in the air. The world below exploded as the Assassin sent liquid evil streaming down at the other Jack from a split second earlier. And though Jack couldn't fly like the Assassin, he could fall as well as anyone. The Assassin destroyed an entire block of the city in his attempt to kill Jack as Jack crashed into him from above.

The Assassin grunted when Jack clung to his neck.

Alexia followed Josiah and the others down a never-ending flight of stairs. "What's this I hear about you being the Child of Prophecy?" Juno asked as they ran.

"What about it?"

"I don't want you thinking we'll be doing any bowing or scraping."

Alexia laughed.

They rounded a corner and ran through a door into a mammoth underground chamber. Thousands of narrow mounds littered the ground. Alexia stumbled. "Are those … graves?" The mounds definitely looked like graves, though each had a small, rounded metal grate at one end.

Juno shook her head as she darted to a nearby lever. An ear-splitting boom echoed through the chamber as the metal grates popped open. One by one, prisoners began crawling out of the narrow mounds.

"They're both prison and grave," Josiah said angrily. "If you die or get sick inside, they seal it up and leave you there."

Thousands of prisoners groaned as they crawled out and stretched cramped muscles. Alexia looked at the mounds again and saw that many had been sealed. "Where are the guards?" She felt ill. How many had died down here while she had been dining on her favorite foods and sleeping in a plush bed?

"I overheard a Shadule say that every dark servant in the city was expected to be in the arena to see you bow before the Assassin," Juno said. "So why did you bow anyway? If you knew you were going to stand with us, why did you give him the satisfaction?"

"Because I didn't know I was going to stand with you until I did it."

"How could you not know?"

"Because I—"

"We don't have time for this." Josiah placed a hand on Alexia's shoulder, and she nodded. "I'll get this lot out," he said. "Juno, you take Alexia to the Clear Eyes. We'll meet you up top."

"What are Clear Eyes?" Alexia asked.

"It's what the Awakened call the animals," Josiah said, "the ones that have chosen to follow the Author. There are at least twenty thousand in the dungeons below."

"Benaiah and Adeline, come with us," Juno said. "Summer, you stay with Josiah. These prisoners are going to need your skills."

Summer nodded and began walking between the prisoners. As she walked, she spread out her arms. Nothing happened that Alexia could see, but she did notice the nearest prisoners began looking somehow ... stronger.

"Are you coming or not?" Juno turned to Alexia.

"I'm coming! I was just ... I'm sorry, Juno. I'm coming." Alexia darted after Juno.

Jack clung to the Assassin as they soared high above the City of Shadows. The Assassin spun and flipped, rocketing forward, but Jack held on. Then the Assassin reached back and wrapped his fingers around Jack's neck. Jack gasped as he tried in vain to tear the sweaty hands away.

No! Darkness formed at the edges of his vision. Then he remembered—and he listened for his note, for the ring of time. Suddenly, Jack and the Assassin rocketed through time, appearing three minutes earlier. They hit the ground, but the Assassin barely noticed the crash landing. He stood and lifted Jack by the neck.

"Nice trick, boy, but your Soulprint will not save you this time!" he snarled.

Jack's vision blurred as he frantically searched for himself. *There!* He met the other Jack's eyes and the other Jack started, then unsheathed Ashandar and dove at the Assassin. At the last second the Assassin dropped Jack and leaped away.

Jack landed on his knees and gasped for breath. As the Assassin rounded on the other Jack, Jack looked himself in the eye and nodded.

"Thank you," he said.

"No worries."

"Shall we end this?"

"I'm ready if you are," the past Jack said fiercely.

Both Jacks felt their blades begin to warm. The Assassin roared. The battle began again.

The Assassin hurled black lightning and torrents of liquid darkness that exploded around them, yet the twin Ashandars deflected the attacks. The Assassin screamed, and as he began to rise, Jack leaped onto his back. Together they flew high into the air—leaving the Jack from the past standing on the ground below.

Arthur could barely find the strength to open his eyes. When he did, he saw a world gone mad. He was lying on cold marble in the center of a narrow passage. A few paces on either side of him, fierce battle raged. Andreal roared as he slammed ax and fist into a wall of dark servants. There were so many of the Shadow Souled and the passageway was so narrow that the bodies were piling up. On Arthur's other side, Mrs. Dumphry sent streams of fire into rank after rank of shrieking attackers.

Wild was lying next to him, leaning heavily against the wall. His eyes were closed and he was covered in dried blood. Arthur touched Wild's knee fearfully, hoping he was still alive. Wild's eyes shot open, and in less than a heartbeat, he was kneeling over Arthur with a blade pressed against his throat.

"You really need to be more careful," Wild said shakily as he made the knife disappear somewhere up his sleeve.

Arthur fingered the tiny cut on his neck. "What's happening?" He groaned. He was so tired he could barely form the words.

"We are holding the stairwell for as long as we can," Wild said. "Alexia has gone with the others to free prisoners from the dungeons below."

Arthur turned to see the darkened stairwell. "Then why are you sleeping?"

"We have no idea how long we will need to hold this corridor," Wild said. "It's so narrow that only two or three of the dark servants can attack at a time, and when they die, their bodies block others from coming. If we save our energy, we should be able to hold it for a while, so we're taking turns. Before you woke me, I was resting." Wild yawned. "I'll switch places with Mrs. Dumphry soon enough."

Arthur could see it now; the corridor was packed to bursting with dark servants, but there were so many that it was working against them. "And Aias?"

"Aias is one floor down, watching the stairs to make sure we aren't attacked from below."

Arthur laid his head back against the floor, letting the exhaustion sink into his bones. "You can really sleep in the middle of all of this?"

Wild grinned. "You've been, haven't you? When you use your Soulprint as strongly as you did, you can sleep for a week. If you aren't careful, you could drop dead from exhaustion. You did well, but right now what you need is rest!"

Arthur did feel more exhausted than ever before. Yet as he watched Andreal slam his fist into an Oriax, he couldn't imagine being able to sleep. Though he might close his eyes for a moment, just to let them rest a bit.

Alexia was surrounded by thousands of animals of every kind—polar bear, giraffe, crocodile, ape, muskrat, koala, moose, dog, ostrich, hippo, panda, elephant, mouse … Every animal Alexia had ever heard of and many she'd never heard of was in this mammoth cavern, each kept in a pen barely large enough for it to stand. Alexia stifled an urge to scream.

"They force the Clear Eyes to fight one another in the arena," Juno said disgustedly. "Those that refuse are killed by Oriax who want to become more powerful. The animals that choose to fight become Oriax or they die." Tears shone in Juno's eyes. "It's horrible."

Alexia felt sick. The Assassin was making animals kill one another so he could grow his army of Oriax. It was too terrible to imagine. She walked over and placed her hand on the trunk of a particularly large elephant. She was only a little surprised to find she knew the animal. Its name was Ollie.

I should have expected it. The Assassin had rounded up every human and animal Alexia had ever interacted with. She wouldn't be surprised if all of the animals from the circus were somewhere in this chamber.

"I'm sorry, Ollie," she whispered. "I am going to get you out of here; I promise."

The elephant wrapped its trunk around Alexia in a sort of elephant hug. She looked at Ollie and felt something stirring; an image formed in her mind's eye, but before she could grasp it, Juno spoke.

"You know this elephant?"

The image dissipated. Alexia shook her head to clear her thoughts. "I do," she said and stepped onto one of Ollie's tusks. "He was one of my very best friends." Ollie lifted her up just as he had back in the circus.

"Your friends have a habit of winding up here."

"It's true," Alexia said sadly. "Let's get them out. All of them."
Alexia scanned the nearest animals and pointed at a large moose and
a particularly savage-looking Bengal tiger. "Those two will be safe,"
she said. "They are wild, but they will not harm you. Climb on and
follow me." Alexia couldn't say how she knew this. There were others
that might have been safer to ride, but these two wanted to help; she
could feel it.

Adeline and Juno looked at her as if she'd gone mad.

"It's one of my Soulprints," she said. "They will not harm you.
They want to fight the Assassin as badly as we do."

"You had better be right," Juno said as she walked to the
Bengal tiger and climbed on. The tiger snarled but seemed content
to let her stay. Adeline watched, wide-eyed, then walked to the
moose. The majestic animal stamped its hooves, then bent its head
low. Adeline grabbed its antlers, and in one smooth motion she was
on its back.

"Okay," Alexia shouted. "It's time to fight back. It's time to
show the Assassin he has not broken us. We are stronger than he
could imagine and we will win this war!" Alexia was sure the animals didn't understand her words, but they did understand that
something was happening. Alexia whispered into Ollie's ear and the
elephant walked over to a thick lever and pulled it with his trunk.

As the door to every cage in the cavern sprung open, Ollie
pushed forward and galloped toward the stairs. Alexia inserted a
stone into her sling; behind her Juno shouted and Adeline squealed
with delight.

Chapter 25

TO LOSE A BATTLE

Ollie rushed up a wide stairwell as Alexia lay low on his back. The ceiling was barely high enough for the elephant to run without hitting his head.

Juno and Adeline followed close, and behind them came a stampede of thousands upon thousands of animals. At the top of the stairwell, Ollie galloped into a mass of dark servants packed into the cramped passageway. The mighty elephant swung his trunk and thrust his tusks as he plowed through the crowd like an avalanche. The Bengal tiger pounced on any dark servant still standing, as Adeline's moose kicked its hind legs and swung its antlers at the creatures.

The Shadow Souled shrieked as the herd charged through them. Ollie crashed down the passage, yet Alexia knew he couldn't keep it up for long. If the elephant slowed, the dark servants would overwhelm him.

Just ahead Alexia saw balls of white flame exploding into the enemy. *Yes!* She whispered encouragement in Ollie's ear as the elephant lunged forward. Within seconds Alexia and her menagerie were standing before Mrs. Dumphry.

Behind Mrs. Dumphry, Andreal battled a never-ending stream of the Shadow Souled. Yet now that Mrs. Dumphry was free, she turned and sent a wall of flame speeding into them. The Shadow Army shrieked as they began to flee the corridor.

Alexia's breath caught when she saw Wild lying with his head against the stone wall. He was incredibly pale and bleeding from multiple wounds. "Is he … Is Wild—" She couldn't finish.

Wild opened his eyes and looked up at her, blinking once, twice. "Took you long enough," he said, and grinned. "I got so tired of waiting I decided to take a nap."

Alexia rolled her eyes. *The boy is impossible*, she thought happily. Arthur was still fast asleep on the stony floor. Just then, Aias appeared in the stairwell. He was followed by Josiah, Summer, Benaiah, and the thousands of prisoners.

Mrs. Dumphry wiped sweat from her brow. "It seems you have found even more of our friends," she said as she observed the Clear Eyes. "There is no time to dally. The Shadow Army is fully conscious, and every one of them is spilling from the arena. If the streets aren't blocked already, they soon will be. Lead us into the streets, my girl," she said to Alexia, "and try to find a way out of this city!"

Alexia felt a rush of adrenaline as she whispered into Ollie's ear. The elephant lurched upward as an image of a raging river bursting through a dam formed in Alexia's mind. She had no idea what it meant, but she was sure the image had come from Ollie. Within seconds they were crashing out of the passageway and into the wall of Shadow Souled who were spilling into the streets.

Thirty minutes later, Alexia was weary beyond words. Ollie had charged through twenty blocks of the enemy. Yet every street was packed, and before long the poor elephant had stumbled and fallen. By the time Ollie rose again, there were far too many dark servants filling the street to continue forward.

Ollie fought valiantly, slamming his tusks into the enemy and kicking them away as Alexia stood on his back and sent stone after stone flying into the never-ending stream of dark servants.

Before long, she was pulled from the elephant's back and had to make use of a sword she'd stolen from one of the Shadow Souled. The fighting was far too cramped to use her sling. Yet no matter how many dark servants she took down, there were always more to come. And inch by inch the army of Awakened was pressed inward as human and animal fell beneath the flood of darkness.

The battle was unlike anything Alexia had imagined. Many of the freed prisoners had Soulprints of their own. Vines sprang up out of nowhere, wrapping around the enemy and flinging them away. Tornadoes of snow and ice blasted through the streets, freezing Shadow Souled in an instant.

Impossible things were happening all around as alleyways filled with crystalline water, gushing into the streets and slamming into the enemy. Walls appeared out of nowhere, surrounding fifty dark servants at a time and locking them inside.

A few animals also seemed to have Soulprints. She saw a zebra turn the front half of its body into stone and smash into the enemy. Then there was an armadillo that grew a metallic shell and curled itself into a ball to roll beneath the Shadow Souled and knock their feet out from under them.

Yet even with five thousand Awakened and twenty thousand animals, it was obvious they would not win this battle. They wouldn't even come close. For every dark servant they dispatched, another hundred remained.

Alexia dispatched a mammoth beast that was part elephant and part octopus. From the corner of her eye, she saw Aias lock blades with the traitor Miel. Alexia hadn't seen the woman since she'd been kidnapped from the palace in London. Miel moved like a viper, but she was no match for Aias. The one-armed warrior spun backward and knocked the woman to the ground.

Something slammed into the middle of the street, drawing Alexia's attention. Stone and dirt went flying as someone let out an impossibly loud scream. For a moment the battle stopped as every dark servant and Awakened turned to see what new evil had arrived. Alexia gaped as she saw the Assassin holding a fresh wound in his side. Sweat poured from him as black blood spilled onto the ground.

Lying on his back before the Assassin was Jack Staples. He was gasping for breath and trying to rise.

Four minutes earlier

The Assassin rocketed through the air as Jack clung to his back. Jack had managed to keep hold of Ashandar in one hand as he wrapped both legs and his other arm around the Assassin. Gritting his teeth, he let go with his arm and held on tightly with his legs, riding the Assassin like a horse. Jack grabbed Ashandar with both hands and was about to stab the Assassin in the back when the Assassin spun like a top. Ashandar flew out of Jack's grasp. He grew dizzy, watching it fall to the city streets far below.

The Assassin hurled Jack across the sky, but he didn't fall far before the Assassin slammed into him, holding him by the neck and placing his other hand over Jack's heart.

The Assassin slowed, then stopped in midair, hovering in the clouds far above the City of Shadows. Jack's heart burned and he felt his life slipping away. The fires from the Assassin's eyes were as hot as a furnace, and a rapturous smile parted his lips.

"This is why you were born, boy," the Assassin said. "This is your purpose. To die at my hands." The area around Jack's heart was on fire as the Assassin dug his fingers into his chest. The edges of his vision darkened. Dimly, Jack heard the ringing of bells and surrendered to them. He had no idea where or when they would go, and he didn't care. At this moment, it was the only way he knew to fight back.

They landed in the Brazilian rain forest. The Assassin glanced at the changed landscape. "No matter where you run, you cannot escape me!" he scoffed. "Your death will end this war, Jack Staples."

Jack hovered on the edge of consciousness. The world grew darker by the second, and he could see little more than the raging fires in the Assassin's eyes.

"But I will not stop with you. I will destroy everyone you know and love. Your father and brother, your friends …"

Wait! Jack had heard these words before. *There!* He saw himself, the Jack from the past. The other Jack wore a blindfold and held Ashandar in both hands. He moved with a fluid grace and twisted the black blade upward—into the Assassin's side. "No!" The Assassin gasped as the Jack from the past screamed "No!" alongside him.

And as the other Jack stumbled and fell, Jack Staples embraced the ring of time and brought the Assassin back to the City of Shadows.

The Assassin dropped Jack and pressed his hands tightly against the fresh wound in his side. Even as he screamed, a dark wind burst from the wound to explode through the streets. And where the wind blew, the Shadow Souled grew stronger.

Only now did Jack realize that he and the Assassin had arrived in the middle of a great battle. The streets were filled with tens of thousands of dark servants battling a small number of human Awakened and a few thousand animals. For a moment it seemed as if the battle had stopped. Every eye was on Jack and the Assassin.

Jack scrambled to his feet and began to run. The Assassin was wounded, but far from dead.

"Kill them all!" the Assassin wailed as entire buildings and streets exploded into flames. Awakened and dark servants alike were buried beneath the rubble as dark fire and liquid evil spread through the streets.

The battle was lost. No matter how valiantly they fought, it wasn't going to be enough. Even before the Assassin arrived, it had been over. With his arrival, the Awakened were falling so quickly it took Alexia's breath away. She closed her eyes and tried to make the Oriax and beasts fall asleep again. She tried to remember what she had done at least twice before, but nothing happened. Even if she had managed it, she knew in her heart it wouldn't be enough.

A short distance down the street, the Assassin walked among the Awakened. "Run, boy!" he screamed as entire streets exploded. "Your time has come!" Shadowfog flooded through the streets to smother the Awakened in its embrace. "This day will mark my final victory!"

Alexia spotted Jack scrambling away, diving behind exploding walls or darting down alleys that erupted in flames. The Assassin was toying with him, laughing each time Jack narrowly escaped yet another attack. Where the Assassin walked, man, woman, and animal were flung aside like rag dolls. Even dark servants unlucky enough to be in his way were destroyed.

Alexia whispered in Ollie's ear, telling him it was time to go after the Assassin. She knew that she and Ollie would be running to their deaths, but she couldn't just watch. Besides, the moment the Assassin killed Jack, he would be coming for her. She was sure of it. She was about to climb onto the elephant's back when she heard a familiar voice.

"I hoped we would meet on the battlefield."

Alexia turned to see Korah pulling his bone-white blade from the body of a mountain goat. "Go!" Alexia hissed. Ollie trumpeted loudly as he bolted away. "Hello, Uncle," she said. "I have been looking for you as well."

Alexia drew her short sword and stepped toward him. Fierce battle raged all around, but man and girl ignored it as they faced each other. Korah grimaced as he raised his blade. "I don't know what I hated more, pretending to be my weakling of a brother or pretending to be your father."

"If it makes you feel better, you weren't good at either," Alexia said. For just a moment, she glanced at something over Korah's shoulder and smiled. Korah shifted his stance so he could look back—

It was all the time Alexia needed. In Korah's moment of distraction, she slung a stone into his hand. Korah screamed as he dropped the blade. Before he could pick up his sword, Alexia had the sling spinning again.

"This is the sling my father gave me." She spoke in a cold voice. "What did you call it? A child's weapon? Since I am the Child of Prophecy, it's fitting that I use a child's weapon to defeat you."

Korah snarled as he shot a wall of black flames toward her. Yet Alexia had already flung her stone, and as she leaped away from the flames, it struck Korah in the forehead, knocking him flat on his back.

Alexia stared down at her uncle. She realized she didn't hate him, but pitied him. Just before she'd released the stone, she'd slowed the spinning of the sling. She didn't want to kill her uncle. Korah was a murderer, and Alexia didn't want to be anything like him.

As she turned to look for the Assassin, her heart sank. The battle was over. The few remaining Awakened were being overwhelmed even as she watched. From every side, man, woman, and animal went down to the dark army. The battle was nearing an end, and the final few hundred Awakened would not last another minute.

We did our best, she thought sadly as she watched a building collapse around Ollie. Yet Alexia could no longer think about the others. Fifty dark servants were rushing toward her. She gritted her teeth and turned to run. If she had any chance of living even a minute longer, it would be because she fought from the rooftops.

She darted toward the nearest building as colored mist rose from the paving stones. A creature with three heads leaped at Alexia, but she dropped at the last moment and rolled beneath it, then leaped to a windowsill. She pulled herself up and kicked at a creature that was nothing but eyeballs, teeth, and matted fur.

Alexia shimmied to the rooftop and turned to send a stone into a lizard-like beast with one head and two bodies. Colored mist now covered the entire street. It surrounded the remnants of the Awakened like a rainbow fog. Alexia stabbed her sword at a monster that had no head, then turned to send a stone into a beast that was a ball of nothing but clawed feet.

She reached inside her cloak for another stone and found the pocket empty. *No!* Five monsters were crawling up the wall as more rocketed down from above. There was nowhere left to go.

Alexia closed her eyes and stepped back. It would be far better to die from a fall than be torn to pieces by the Shadow Souled. *This is the end*, she thought as she fell backward through the air. A strange peace rose inside her as memories flooded her mind. She was three years old and climbing a large boulder outside her house. Her father ran over and hugged her fiercely. "You climb better than a mountain goat!" he said with a grin. She was four, and her mother taught her how to tie a sailor's knot. "You are very good at that, my girl," she said as she wrapped Alexia in a hug.

There were tears of joy in Alexia's eyes. These memories were what life was about—family and love and joy and laughter. These moments were what gave meaning to her life. She was five and sitting on her parents' bed, opening her presents. Her parents laughed so hard that they began to cry. She was seven and jumping about with her friends in the Gang of Rogues, whooping and hollering. Alexia was thirteen and sitting with Megan Staples, drinking tea and eating strawberry pie. All of the painful and heartbreaking moments of her life faded as she remembered the people she loved and who loved her back.

All these memories and more flooded through her in the blink of an eye. And as she fell, she braced herself. Yet she didn't hit the ground. Alexia thought she might be hallucinating when she saw she had landed on top of a large red fox with wide wings. That's when she saw the Sephari. There were at least fifty of them, hovering above the street. Spinning wildly above them was an unearthly tornado.

Paving stones, gargoyles, roofs of buildings, and even dark servants rose from the ground to spin in the ever-growing cyclone. Many of the winged Shadow Souled had also been drawn into it.

"Elion!" Alexia breathed. Elion's eyes blazed like the sun, and as she began to sing, all of the Sephari joined in. It was the most terrifying and awesome thing Alexia had ever heard, as if fifty different songs had somehow joined together to form a masterpiece. It was a cadence, a war cry, and a mournful dirge—and it was absolutely breathtaking.

Alexia remembered Elion's song from the battle in the square of Buckingham Palace. She remembered thinking it had been the most beautiful thing in the world. Yet it was nothing compared to this. This song had power, as if the song itself were alive and taking part in the battle.

Besides the fifty Sephari and their fearsome song, Alexia saw at least six more winged animals. In the air nearby was a lion, a meerkat, a rather large rabbit, and a panther. More beasts circled farther off, though she could barely see them through the thickening hurricane spinning above the Sephari.

What are they waiting for? Alexia wondered. The Awakened were growing fewer by the second. Even with the arrival of the Sephari, the dark servants had barely slowed their attack. Alexia saw Josiah and Juno standing back-to-back and striking out with sword and spear at Petrus, the Gang of Terror, and row upon row of dark servants that surrounded them; Adeline was lying unconscious on the ground between them.

A mountain of bodies ringed Mrs. Dumphry, but thousands more were scrambling to get to her. Aias lay unmoving at her feet with a spear protruding from his chest. Jack had found his black sword and was wielding it with a master's hand. He danced among thirty of the Shadow Souled, spinning and twisting the blade with a deadly fury, yet she had no doubt he would be overwhelmed in a few more seconds. The Assassin was there, though at the moment his attention was on the Sephari above. Liquid evil shot upward to explode against shields of light.

Abruptly, the Sephari's song ended as Elion threw down her arms. A hail of marble, diamonds, gemstone, gold, paving stones, barrels, dark servants, and rooftops rocketed toward the ground.

The army of Shadow Souled shrieked in fear as death rained down to smash them away from the few Awakened still standing. Much of the debris crashed into the Assassin, quickly burying him beneath a mountain of rubble. For a moment the street was still. The few Awakened still standing looked toward the heavens in exhaustion.

The attack from the Sephari had been deadly, though it had bought the Awakened only a few seconds at most. The rubble covering the Assassin was already shifting and falling away, and the Shadow Souled from the surrounding streets were spilling in.

As the flying animals swooped down and gathered the remnants, Alexia wept. Barely a handful was still standing and not one member of her Gang of Rogues was among them.

Jack looked numbly down upon the City of Shadows. Thousands of humans and animals had been left behind. *No!* His eyes found Aias. The last he'd seen, the one-armed man had been fighting fifty Shadow Souled at once. Now he lay among the rubble with a spear in his chest, his eyes staring blankly at the heavens. Aias had been one of the first humans to Awaken. And now he was gone.

When he had first seen the Sephari and the flying animals, he'd hoped more were coming. He hoped they could take everyone, but he had been wrong. From what Jack could see, only Alexia, Mrs. Dumphry, Wild, Andreal, and Arthur had been saved, though Arthur was unconscious atop the winged meerkat.

Jack turned to look at Alexia. *At least she is safe.* It was a numb thought. As their eyes met, they nodded. *She's my sister!* Jack still could barely believe it. He clung to the back of the panther as a chill passed through him.

"I am sorry, Jack. We arrived as quickly as we could, but even if we had come sooner, we wouldn't have been able to save them all." Elion was flying beside Jack and looked as forlorn and exhausted as he felt.

"I know," he said tiredly. "Thank you for saving us. Are the rest of them ..." Jack hesitated, not sure he wanted to hear the answer. "Are they all dead?"

"I don't know," Elion said. "But there is nothing we can do for them now."

Jack wiped fresh tears from his eyes.

"The Assassin thought he would win the war today. Yet in a single battle he lost both of the Children of Prophecy. He will be angry." Elion shivered. "And that will make him even more danger-ous. But you did well. You wounded him for the second time, and that is no small thing."

"Will we win?" Jack asked. "In the end, will we be able to stand against him?"

"I do not know," Elion said. "I don't think he could ever kill the Author as he plans, but he may be powerful enough to destroy the world. Yet we must stand and fight no matter the outcome."

Jack stared at the darkening sky. "What happens now?" He suddenly felt cold.

"The Last Battle has begun, and nothing in all of creation will be able to stand aside. The choice will be made—the Author or the Assassin." Elion's eyes turned as black as pitch. "The world has become a far more dangerous place. Every blade of grass, every insect and mountain, even the air itself will become enemy or ally. We must gather every last Awakened into an army like this world has never known. And we must find the Poet's Coffer. Without it, we have no chance of standing against the coming darkness."

Jack clung to the panther as they flew over rivers and valleys. He had no idea what the Poet's Coffer was, and at the moment he didn't care. So many of the Awakened had been lost in a single battle! Right now all he wanted was to sleep.

As Jack Staples closed his eyes and fell into a fitful sleep, his sister, Alexia Dreager, also slept atop her stallion. And as the Children of Prophecy flew toward the horizon, neither saw the mountains tremble or the valleys quake. Neither Jack nor Alexia witnessed the sinkholes forming below, swallowing entire forests in a matter of seconds. Neither child noticed the grass of the fields withering as large swathes of earth chose to follow the Assassin.

The Last Battle had begun, and the choice was being made. And the world itself began to tremble.

Chapter 26

AN UNEXPECTED VISITOR

Three hours later

Alexia didn't make a sound as the Shadule threw the five members of her Gang of Rogues into the prison cell. All looked weary beyond words and carried multiple wounds. She stayed safely hidden in the darkened corner of the cell, barely able to contain her excitement.

"The master will come for you soon," the Shadule rasped. "You will beg for death by the time he is done."

None of Alexia's friends protested as the Shadule closed the prison door. Juno dropped to the cold, wet floor and cradled Adeline's head in her lap. Adeline was bleeding from a wound in her shoulder. Josiah stared blankly at the closed door as Summer and Benaiah sat beside him. All five were filthy and streaked in blood; some of the blood was theirs, much of it was not.

Alexia waited until she was sure the Shadule was gone, then stepped out from the darkness. "I know you are weary," she said boldly, "but if you are willing to come with me, I can get you out of here. And with your help, we can free every last prisoner and animal."

None of the children so much as moved.

"I don't ..." Josiah stopped. "We saw you fly away ..."

"I did," Alexia agreed, "but that was three weeks ago. I've come from the past to rescue you." A boy stepped out from the shadows behind her. "This is Parker Staples. He'll help us. But before we free the prisoners, I'm going to need your help with something else." Alexia was giddy with excitement. "We're going to free my mother."

Read on for an exciting excerpt from the final book in this series,
Jack Staples and the Poet's Storm.

The wonder of riding a flying fox had faded long ago. Although the varmint was graceful, spending two days on its back with little sleep or chance to stretch her legs had left Alexia Dreager incredibly sore. She'd named the fox Dagger because of the way he flew. Dagger had an impressive ability to shift direction and dart about without warning.

Alexia hugged Dagger close as he dove straight down and turned sharply to the left. Her fists tightened on the handfuls of fur as the fox soared toward the face of an enormous bluff. Alexia squealed in delight as her winged friend twisted sideways and entered a hidden cavern. Dagger had the precision of an eagle and the agility of a sparrow. The fox flipped upright as he glided in, then dropped and skidded to a stop, sending dust and shale flying.

Alexia exhaled heavily before climbing from his back. Every muscle burned and she was weary beyond words, yet she took the time to scratch Dagger behind the ears before stretching. The fox had to be even wearier than Alexia. *You did well.* She sent the thought as Dagger yawned widely. She cleared her mind and waited, but nothing came as the poor beast collapsed in exhaustion.

Alexia had spent much of the past two days trying to communicate with Dagger. It was the strangest thing she'd ever done, and she still wasn't sure it was actually happening. More than once, an image had formed unbidden in her mind, and she was certain the images had come from Dagger. *I just need to learn how to understand what the images mean,* she thought. *And to figure out how to make him understand me!*

Alexia turned to watch as more flying beasts entered the cavern, each landing with varying degrees of grace. A winged black panther came first, carrying a bleary-eyed Jack Staples. Next came an overly large meerkat with Wild atop, followed by a winged beaver with Arthur Greaves still asleep on its back. Alexia could barely believe it; the boy had slept through most of the past two days, waking only to eat or relieve himself.

Next came a very large and very beleaguered winged rabbit, lugging the giant, Andreal. Every time Alexia saw Andreal climb onto the hare's back, the poor animal let out an audible sigh before launching into the air. Last came Mrs. Dumphry's tusked elephant, its two sets of wings scraping the side of the cavern. The ancient Mrs. Dumphry hadn't been herself these past two days. Aias, the man she'd loved for more then five thousand years, had been killed in the City of Shadows.

Her friends climbed off their rides and then stretched, their muscles tired from the journey. The rest of the Clear Eyes, the animals that had chosen to serve the Author, collapsed in exhaustion.

"I do not understand," Andreal rumbled. He stretched his arms high, his fingers brushing the cavern ceiling. "We should be losing them ages ago; how be it they still be finding us?" He collapsed onto the cavern floor. Andreal reminded Alexia of a bear she'd once known back at the circus.

"A tired body can betray even the most willing mind," Mrs. Dumphry said wearily. "I do not know how they continue to follow, yet I am sure the answer is simple. I am just too weary to see it."

Some version of this conversation came up each time they'd stopped over the past two days. Ten thousand of the Assassin's deadliest warriors had been pursuing them ever since they'd escaped the City of Shadows. At first, Mrs. Dumphry hadn't been worried. She was sure the Clear Eyes could fly faster than the Shadow Souled's winged beasts, yet no matter how fast the Clear Eyes had gone, they'd been unable to stay more than a few hours ahead of the dark army.

Alexia was as vexed as the others, but for different reasons. On the day they escaped the Assassin's city, she'd learned something so incredible she could still barely believe it. Her mother might still be alive. Until then, she'd been sure her mother had passed away when Alexia was just five years old. She had no way of knowing for certain, but it was possible that Madeleine Dreager was out there somewhere.

Yet it wasn't just hope for her mother that occupied Alexia's thoughts. Each hour spent fleeing the dark army took them farther away from the City of Shadows. With each passing hour, Alexia's guilt and misery grew. Though she and a few of her friends had been rescued, Alexia's best friends—her Gang of Rogues—had been left behind. *It's the second time I've abandoned them;* she shivered at the thought.

Her friends were most likely being tortured and starved. *If they're still alive,* she thought coldly. She had no way of knowing who had survived the battle or if the Assassin would bother keeping any of the prisoners alive. The Last Battle had begun, and what need did the Assassin have of prisoners? Alexia didn't care about being the Child of Prophecy or what the Awakened expected of her. The only things that mattered were finding her mother and saving her friends.

She hadn't told anyone what she'd learned about her mother. In part because there had been very little time to talk since their escape, and in part because she was afraid to. Although she no longer hated Mrs. Dumphry, she still didn't know what to think of the woman. But more than anything, she was certain Mrs. Dumphry would never allow her to run off. *I am one of the Children of Prophecy, after all*, she thought glumly. The conundrum was that Alexia had no idea where to look for her mother or how to save her friends, and the only person she could think of to ask for help was Mrs. Dumphry.

Even if I knew where Mother was or could sneak back to the City of Shadows, can I do any of it by myself? She'd spent many years on her own, but that had been in a very different world than the one she was in now. Mrs. Dumphry said the Last Battle had begun and that all of creation was making its choice—the Author or the Assassin. From Dagger's back, Alexia had seen things she still didn't understand. The trees of an entire forest had thrashed about as if fighting one another. Later she'd seen a lake turn as black as pitch within seconds, sending the smell of death high into the air. Alexia had counted five earthquakes in the past two days, and Dagger had needed to fly around a number of tornadoes.

There was something wrong with the weather. It was as if the natural progression of things had been interrupted. Winter leads to spring, spring to summer, and summer to fall. It's this rhythm that allows land to bear fruit and soil to grow rich. Yet over the past two days, it was as if the weather had forgotten its place and there was no rhyme or reason for what happened between one hour and the next. The small band of Awakened had flown through a blizzard straight into a heat wave.

"Where are we?" a voice said from behind her. Alexia turned to see Arthur Greaves awake and standing beside the sleeping winged beaver. "You look horrible!" Arthur gasped as he met Alexia's eyes. "You should really get some sleep or something. I feel great! I've had the craziest dreams you can imagine. We were all riding on the backs of flying—" Arthur stopped as his eyes landed on the beaver. "Wait. What?" He squinted at the other beasts, then grinned. "That's amazing! Is that how we escaped the City of Shadows? The last thing I remember is seeing Andreal and Mrs. Dumphry fighting in the corridors of the coliseum. And where is Elion? Is she here too, or was that just a dream? She was flying beside me for a time. And what happened to the rest of the prisoners? Did everyone get out? I can't believe animals can fly! Jack, did you ever imagine such a thing?"

"Arthur Greaves," Mrs. Dumphry said tiredly, "it's time you learned to tame your tongue. An untamed tongue is far more dangerous than an untrained sword." Mrs. Dumphry sighed as Arthur blushed. She let out an annoyed harrumph, then walked over and placed a hand on his shoulder. "It is good to see you awake, child. You've been sleeping for two days and much has happened. I am sure your friends will catch you up, but right now I need silence if I am to think."

Arthur's jaw dropped. "Two days," he mouthed as Jack placed a hand on his shoulder and walked him toward the back of the cavern. Jack quietly began explaining what Arthur had missed. Arthur squealed at something Jack said, and Alexia couldn't help but smile. She'd once thought the boy to be a coward, but she'd been wrong. He did have the habit of squealing like a little girl and his stomach was weaker than most, but he was no coward. Arthur Greaves had single-handedly saved every one of them from the arena in the City of Shadows. The memory was clear in her mind.

Alexia and the others had been buried beneath a mountain of one hundred thousand Shadow Souled. Then in walked Arthur Greaves. *No,* Alexia remembered, *in danced Arthur Greaves.* Liquid light flowed around him, forming a wall that plowed through the mountain of dark flesh.

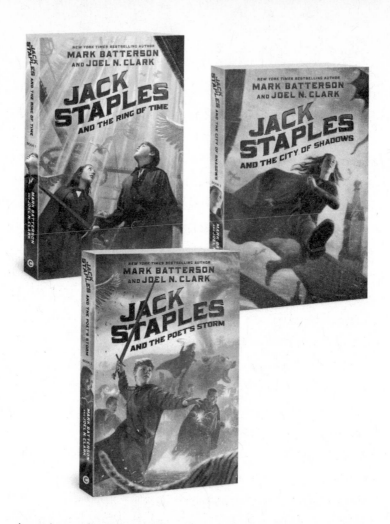

Imagine a far more fantastical world than the one you know—a world that boils just beneath the surface of your ordinary life, if only you have the eyes to see it. This world is filled with giants, time travel, terrifying beast, and mythical creatures that have been at war since before time. Now, imagine you awake to this reality and learn you are at the center of it all; you are destined to both save the world and destroy it. These are the stories of Jack Staples and Alexia Dreager.

DAVID C COOK

transforming lives together